BRAIN G

kids

Amazing Activity Book

Phoenix International Publications, Inc.

Chicago • London • New York • Hamburg • Mexico City • Paris • Sydney

Illustrations: Robin Boyer, Karen Stormer Brooks, Peter Brosshauser, Mattia Cerato, Garry Colby, Mike Dammer, Dave Garbot, Dani Jones, Larry Jones, Kevin Kelly, Robbie Short, Jamie Smith, Chuck Whelon, K Kreto/Shutterstock.com (pattern on cover)

Phoenix International Publications, Inc.
8501 West Higgins Road   59 Gloucester Place
Chicago, Illinois 60631   London W1U 8JJ

Permission is never granted for commercial purposes.

www.pikidsmedia.com

p i kids is a trademark of Phoenix International Publications, Inc., and is registered in the United States.

ISBN: 978-1-5037-4591-9

Manufactured in China.

8 7 6 5 4 3 2 1

LET THE PUZZLE FUN BEGIN!

Do you enjoy finding your way through a twisting and turning maze?

How about creating fun and wacky doodles?

And what about connecting numbered dots to reveal cool scenes?

With *Brain Games Kids: Amazing Activity Book*, you can do all that—and more!

Every page of this book is like a brand-new adventure. One minute you're leading the alien Goob through the cosmos in a zigzagging maze, the next you're searching for spooky words hidden in a scary word search. Sometimes there are multiple puzzles on a page, and sometimes there is just one large puzzle to tackle. No need to worry if you happen to get stuck; just turn to the back of the book and find the answer you need there.

Are you ready? Turn the page and dive into your first puzzle adventure—the first of many!

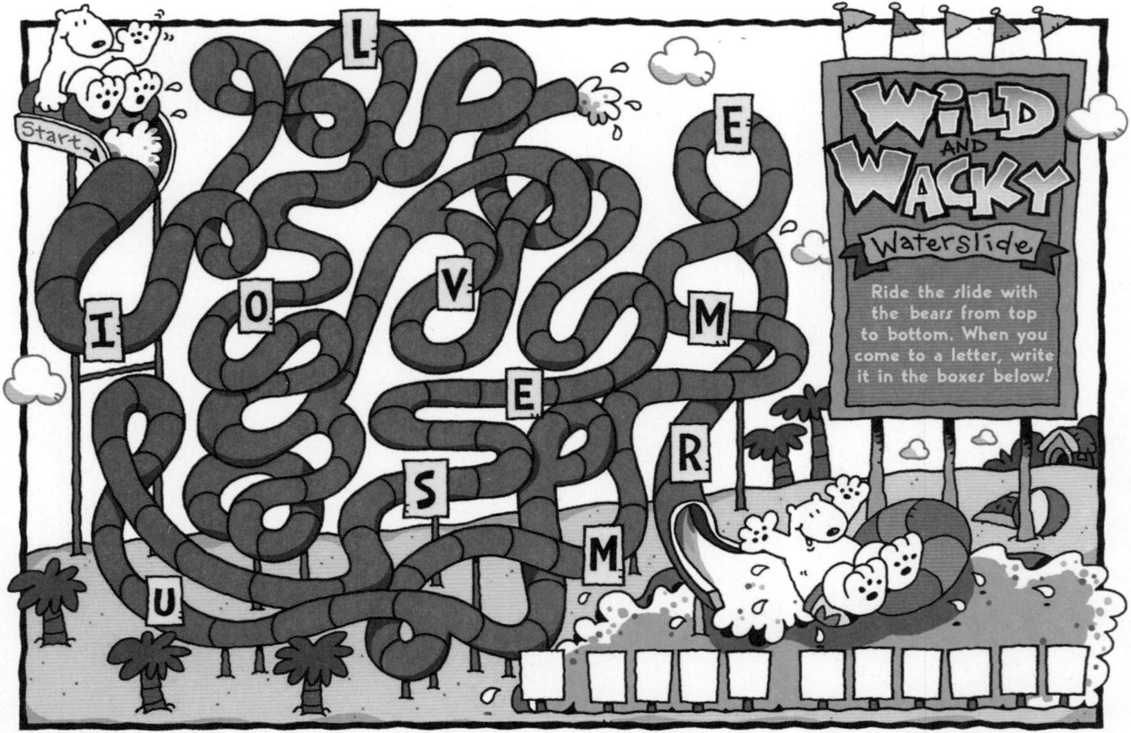
WILD AND WACKY
Waterslide
Ride the slide with the bears from top to bottom. When you come to a letter, write it in the boxes below!
Start
L
E
I
O
V
M
E
R
S
M
U

Answers on page 123.

AbraCaDabra
Can you find these hidden objects within this picture?
banana
cup
butterfly
button
pencil
Can you spot the 10 differences between the rabbits in the hats?
START
END

Answers on page 123.

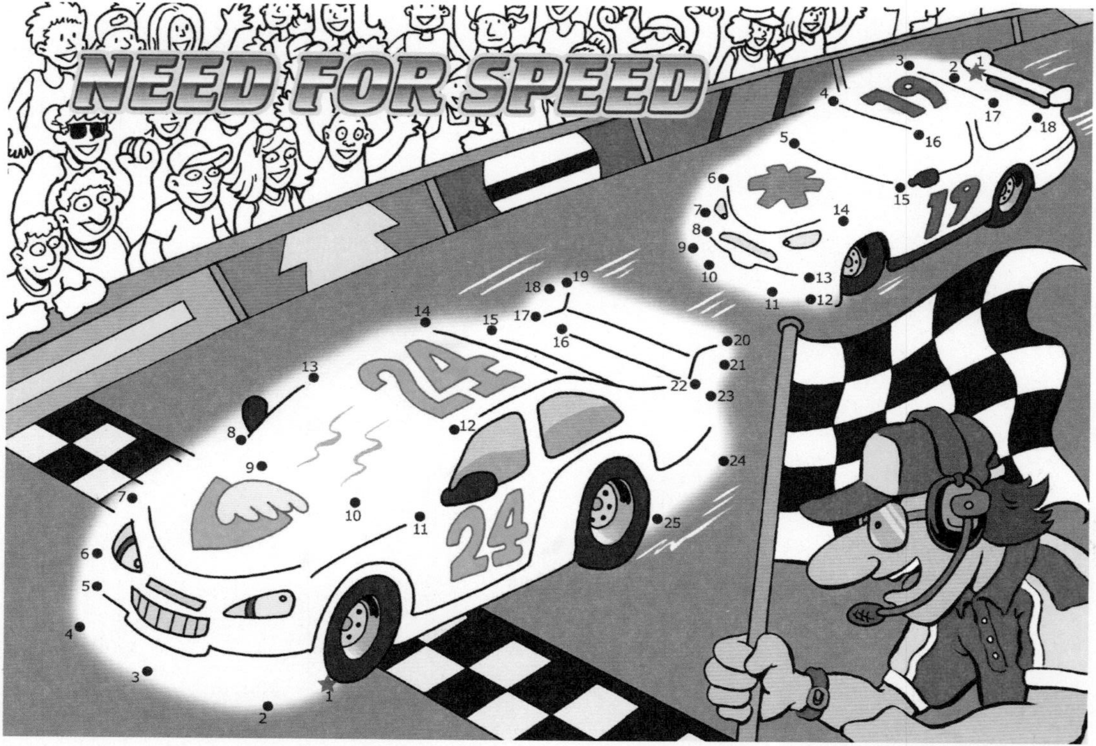

Answers on page 123.

Rain Forest Friends

Complete the baby jaguar and baby gorilla in this scene. Then draw other plants or animals you might find in the rain forest.

Library Challenge

Whoa! This is a BIG library!
Doors with the same letter connect and will lead you up, down, or across.
Make your way from the front steps to the study hall on the top floor!

C	I	S	U	M	E	H
A	D	N	L	P	I	G
S	I	G	N	S	N	S
T	F	Z	T	I	E	R
U	G	O	D	V	N	E
D	R	A	L	R	A	T
Y	E	E	A	P	I	U
R	H	T	A	H	R	P
S	K	U	Z	O	A	M
K	O	C	G	T	R	O
A	S	K	O	O	B	C
U	N	E	T	S	I	L
Q	U	I	E	T	L	B

WORD SEARCH

BOOKS, COMPUTERS, HISTORY, LIBRARIAN, LISTEN, MUSIC, PHOTOS, QUIET, READING, SHELVES, SIGNS, STUDY

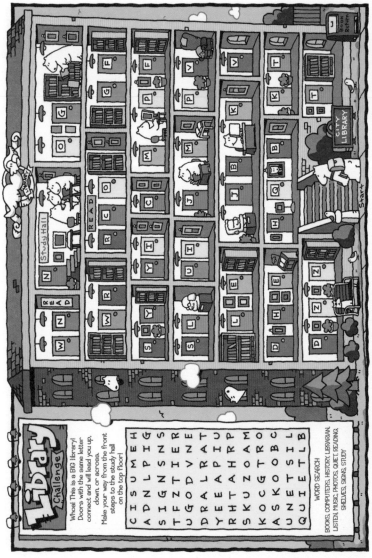

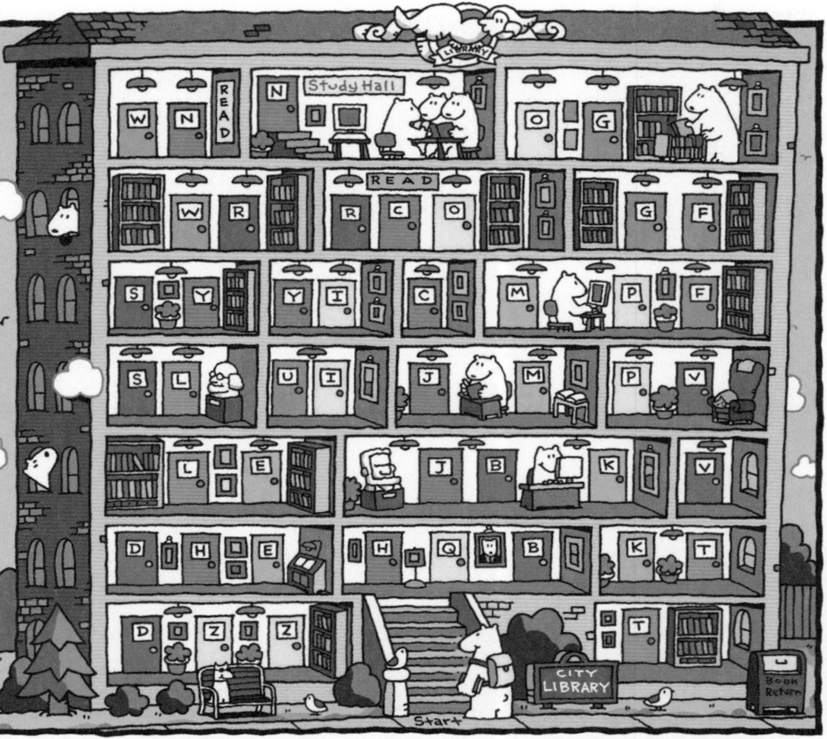

Answers on page 123.

Answers on page 124.

VISITORS FROM outer space

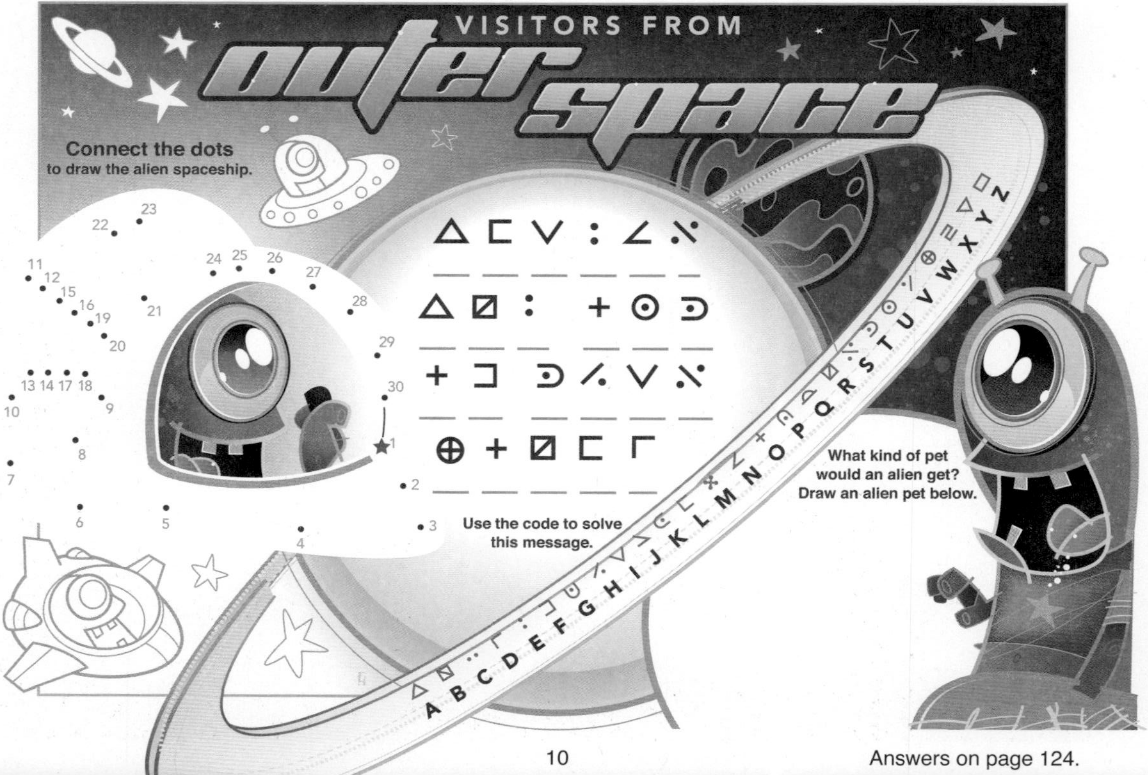
Connect the dots
to draw the alien spaceship.
Use the code to solve
this message.
What kind of pet
would an alien get?
Draw an alien pet below.
A B C D E F G H I J K L M N O P Q R S T U V W X Y Z

Answers on page 124.

LINK THE DOTS
Find the hidden figure.
ALL THE WAY UP IN THE SKY
Look at the skyscrapers.
Which is the tallest?
Which is the shortest?
BRIDGE MAZE
Make your way over the bridge to get to the other side.
START
FINISH
A DAY IN THE CITY
BRIDGE
CITY
Where's the driver going, toward the city or the bridge? Have fun coloring him as you like!
Of all these houses, only two are exactly alike. Can you find them?

Answers on page 124.

Tookie Bird Safari
START
Help the explorers find the sneaky Tookie Bird.
FINISH

Answers on page 124.

MECHANICAL DRAWINGS

Draw this robot in six easy steps. Make lots of robots, or draw a futuristic scene around your mechanical friend for even more doodle fun.

What's the Message?

Use the code to fill in the letters on the lines below to reveal a message just for you!

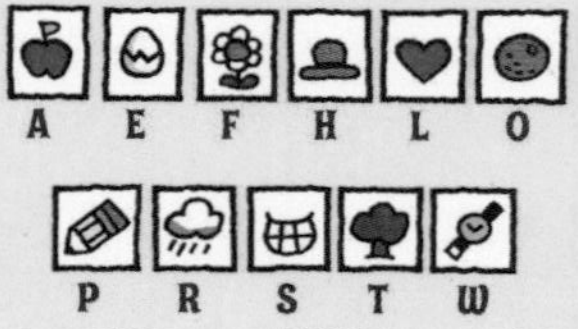

Back to the Hive!

This honeybee is lost in the garden. Help him find his way back to the hive by tracing the correct blue line.

Answers on page 125.

Answers on page 125.

The Wild West
Which hat appears the most along this border?
Which of these two rootin'-tootin' cowpokes roped the moon? Who roped the sun?

Answers on page 125.

Butterfly Flutter

Finish the rest of this butterfly, using the first half as a guide.

Answers on page 125.

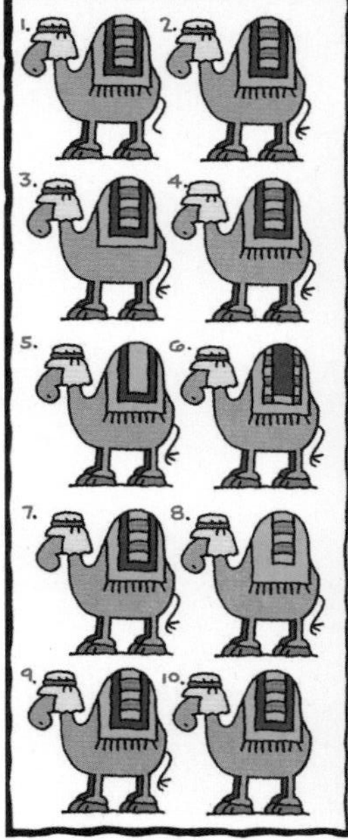

OH MUMMY!

This mummy went on a trip, but he can't remember how to get home! Help him find his way, but first stop at the grocery store and then at the vet to pick up his pooch.

Start

VET

Grocery

Finish

FIND THE TWO CAMELS THAT MATCH!

1. 2. 3. 4. 5. 6. 7. 8. 9. 10.

19

Answers on page 126.

SPORTS Matchup
Doodle the object that is used with each piece of sports equipment shown. For example, a baseball is used with a mitt.

Answers on page 126.

Finish
BIG TOP
challenge!
THE FLYING BEARS ARE READY TO PERFORM, BUT ONE OF THEIR MEMBERS IS STILL ON THE GROUND!
HELP THIS BEAR CHOOSE THE RIGHT ROPE FOR HIS CLIMB UP TOP!
The HUMAN Cannon BALL!
FLYING BEARS
FLY BEA
NO WAY!
FLEA
10
FLYING BEARS
Find
Start

Answers on page 126.

IN THE AGE OF DINOSAURS

There are 10 dinosaur eggs scattered throughout this picture. Can you find them?
Can you find the 10 differences between these 2 pictures?
1 2 3 4 5 6 7 8 9 10 11 12 13 14 15 16 17 18
Connect the dots to see what's coming out of the egg!

Answers on page 126.

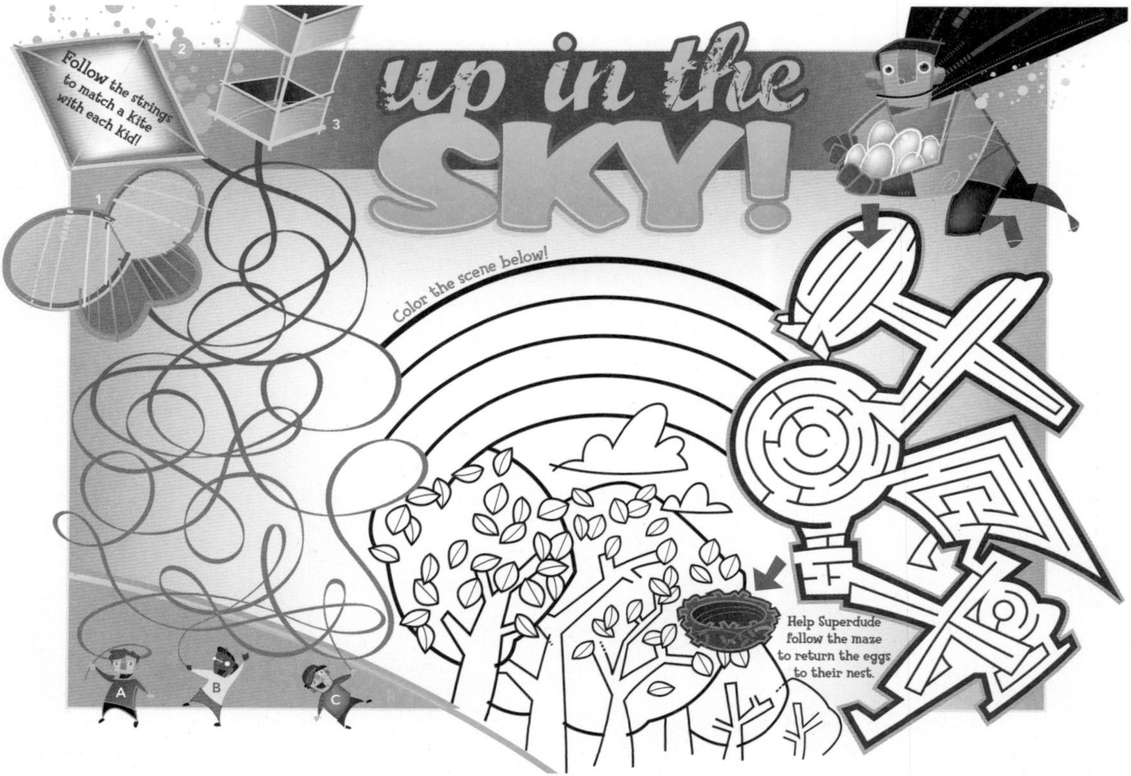
up in the SKY!
Follow the strings to match a Kite with each Kid!
1
2
3
A
B
C
Color the scene below!
Help Superdude follow the maze to return the eggs to their nest.

Answers on page 127.

Answers on page 127.

Fe-Fi-Fo-FUM!
Help this poor giant get his goose back from that THIEVIN' JACK!
START
(Don't cross any yellow lines!)
FINISH!
Unscramble these Fairy-Tale Folks!
INREDLACEL
ETH HETER TILELT SIGP
LIPEGESN TAYEBU
TREEP NAP
IHOPCOINC
NWSO THEWI
HEMROT OSOGE
YTMUPH PUDTYM
EHT IGB DBA FOWL

Answers on page 127.

Toy Shelf
THESE TOYS ARE LOOKING A LITTLE LONELY. DOODLE SOME FRIENDS TO KEEP THEM COMPANY ON THE SHELF UNTIL PLAYTIME BEGINS AGAIN!

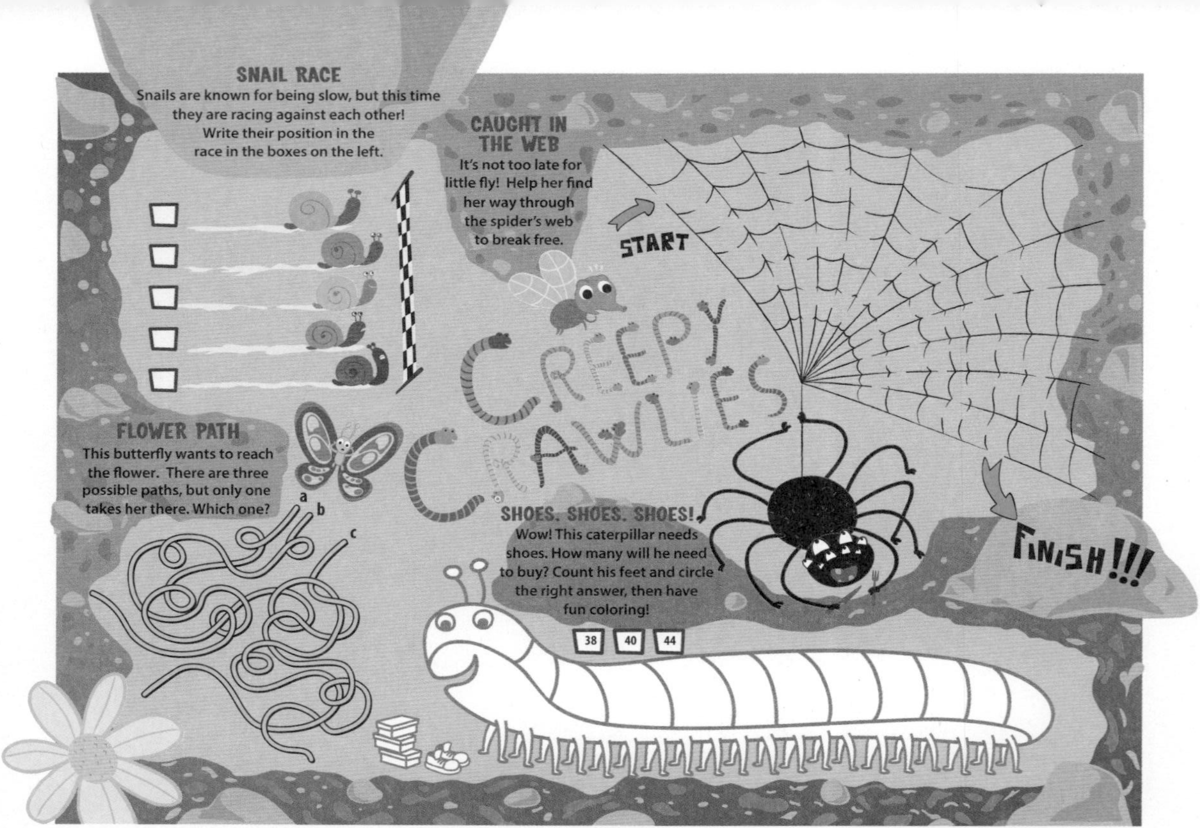
CREEPY CRAWLIES
SNAIL RACE
Snails are known for being slow, but this time they are racing against each other! Write their position in the race in the boxes on the left.
CAUGHT IN THE WEB
It's not too late for little fly! Help her find her way through the spider's web to break free.
START
FINISH!!!
FLOWER PATH
This butterfly wants to reach the flower. There are three possible paths, but only one takes her there. Which one?
a
b
c
SHOES. SHOES. SHOES!
Wow! This caterpillar needs shoes. How many will he need to buy? Count his feet and circle the right answer, then have fun coloring!
38
40
44

Answers on page 127.

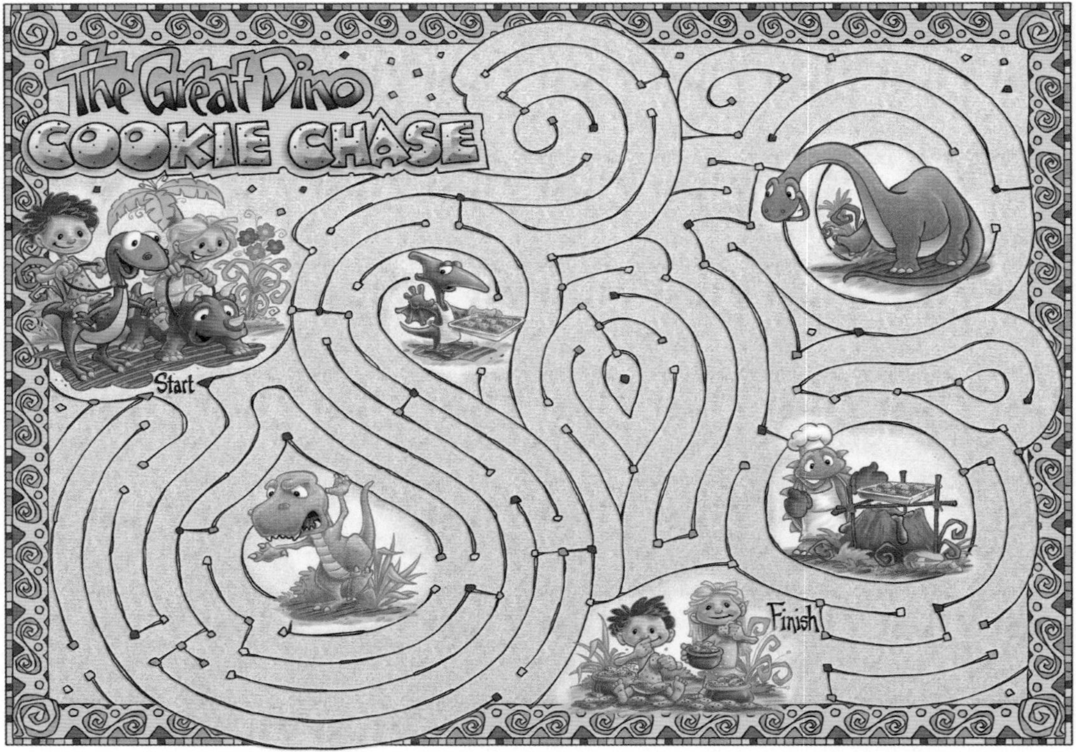

Answers on page 128.

Answers on page 128.

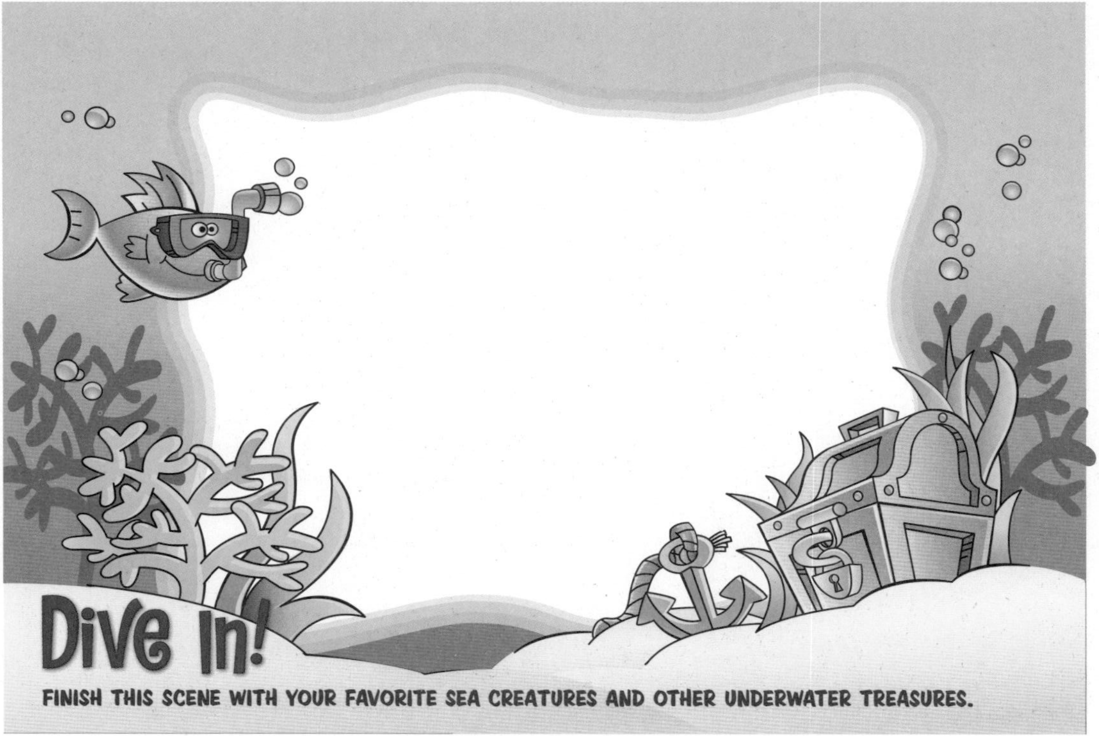
Dive In!
FINISH THIS SCENE WITH YOUR FAVORITE SEA CREATURES AND OTHER UNDERWATER TREASURES.

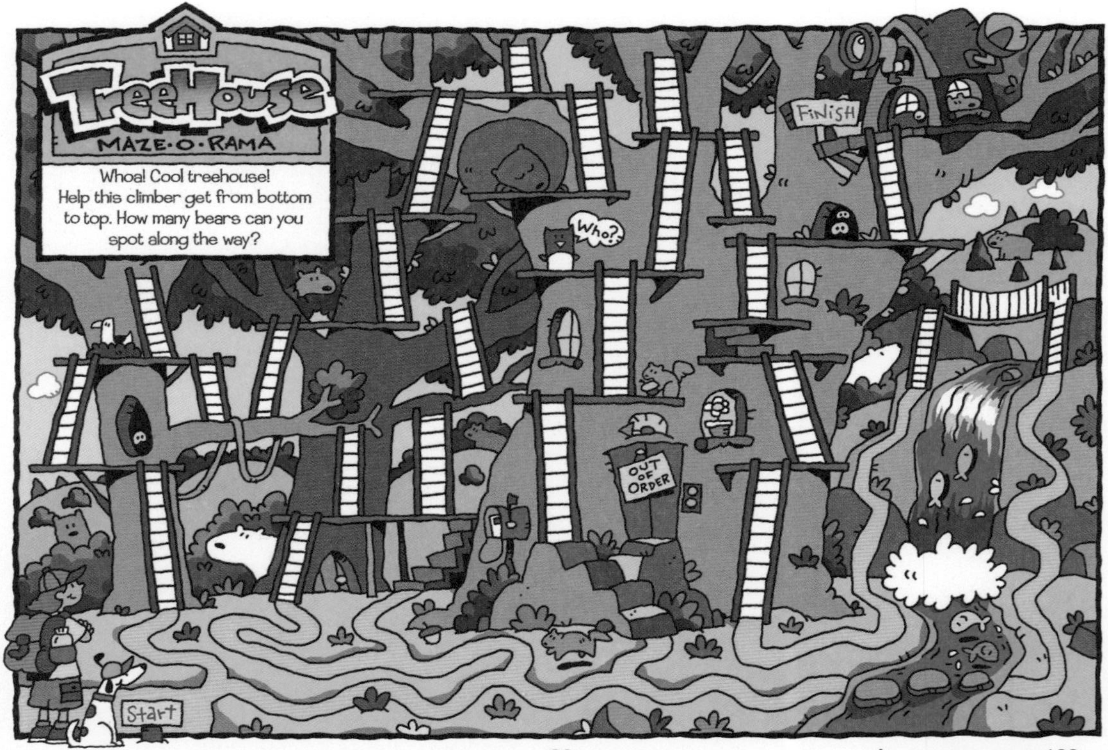
TreeHouse
MAZE·O·RAMA
Whoa! Cool treehouse!
Help this climber get from bottom to top. How many bears can you spot along the way?
Who?
FINISH
OUT OF ORDER
Start

Answers on page 128.

A Trip to the Zoo
YIKES! THE ANIMALS HAVE TAKEN LETTERS FROM SIGNS AROUND THE ZOO! PLEASE MATCH THE LETTER TO EACH ANIMAL IN THE BLANKS TO ANSWER THIS QUESTION: WHAT DO DOLPHINS WEAR TO KEEP WARM?
S
E
P
L
I
F
R
CAN YOU FIND THE ONE CAMEL THAT MATCHES THIS SHADOW EXACTLY?
CHANGE ONE LETTER PER WORD TO TRANSFORM THIS SWEET LITTLE DEER INTO A FEROCIOUS LION!!
DEER
TERM OF AFFECTION
SHAKESPEARE KING
TO REST ON
TO LEND MONEY
LARGE WATERBIRD
LION

Answers on page 128.

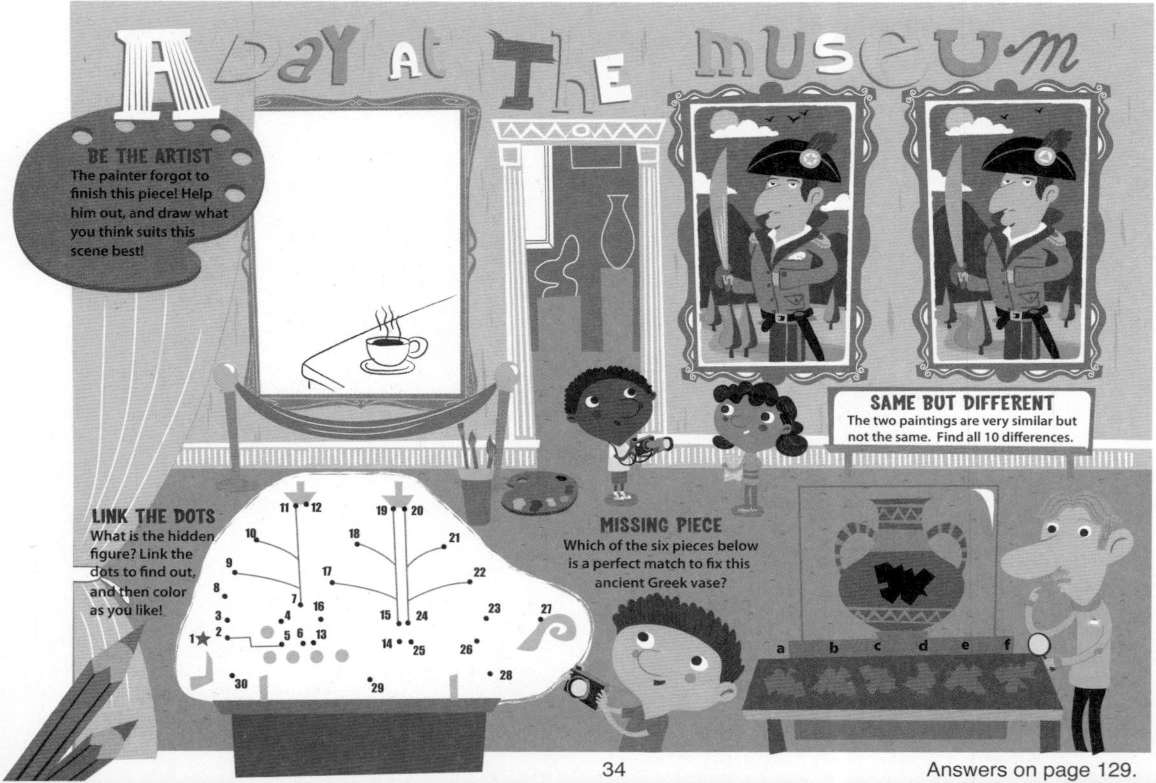
A DAY AT THE MUSEUM
BE THE ARTIST
The painter forgot to finish this piece! Help him out, and draw what you think suits this scene best!
SAME BUT DIFFERENT
The two paintings are very similar but not the same. Find all 10 differences.
LINK THE DOTS
What is the hidden figure? Link the dots to find out, and then color as you like!
1 2 3 4 5 6 7 8 9 10 11 12 13 14 15 16 17 18 19 20 21 22 23 24 25 26 27 28 29 30
MISSING PIECE
Which of the six pieces below is a perfect match to fix this ancient Greek vase?
a b c d e f

Answers on page 129.

Answers on page 129.

ROAD TRIP MAZE

These three New York City bears are driving across the USA to Los Angeles! They want to visit six other cities along the way. The cities are listed below, but not in the right order. Write the names of the cities in the correct order the bears will visit them. Then help them find their way to LA!

1 ____________

2 ____________

3 ____________

4 ____________

5 ____________

6 ____________

New Orleans, Dallas, Chicago, Denver, Seattle, Nashville

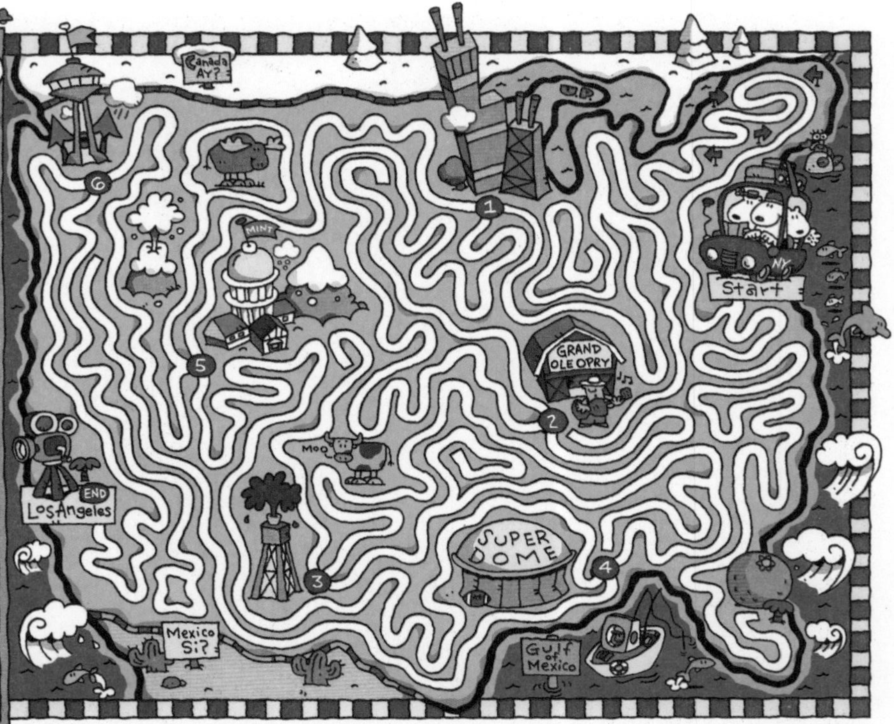

Answers on page 129.

SNOW DAY!

Find matching snowflakes around the page, then find the one-of-a-kind snowflake.

Starting at the arrow, follow the letters sideways, down, or diagonally to reveal a winter phrase.

L	E	B	O	A	V	P	T	L	X
V	P	T	L	X	O	I	T	R	E
O	I	T	R	E	U	R	S	I	P
U	R	S	I	P	K	H	N	O	W
K	H	N	O	W					

BUILD A SNOWMAN!
Find the following objects in the scene below, then draw them on the snowman: two black eyes, three buttons, carrot, scarf, top hat, two stick arms, six circles for mouth.

37

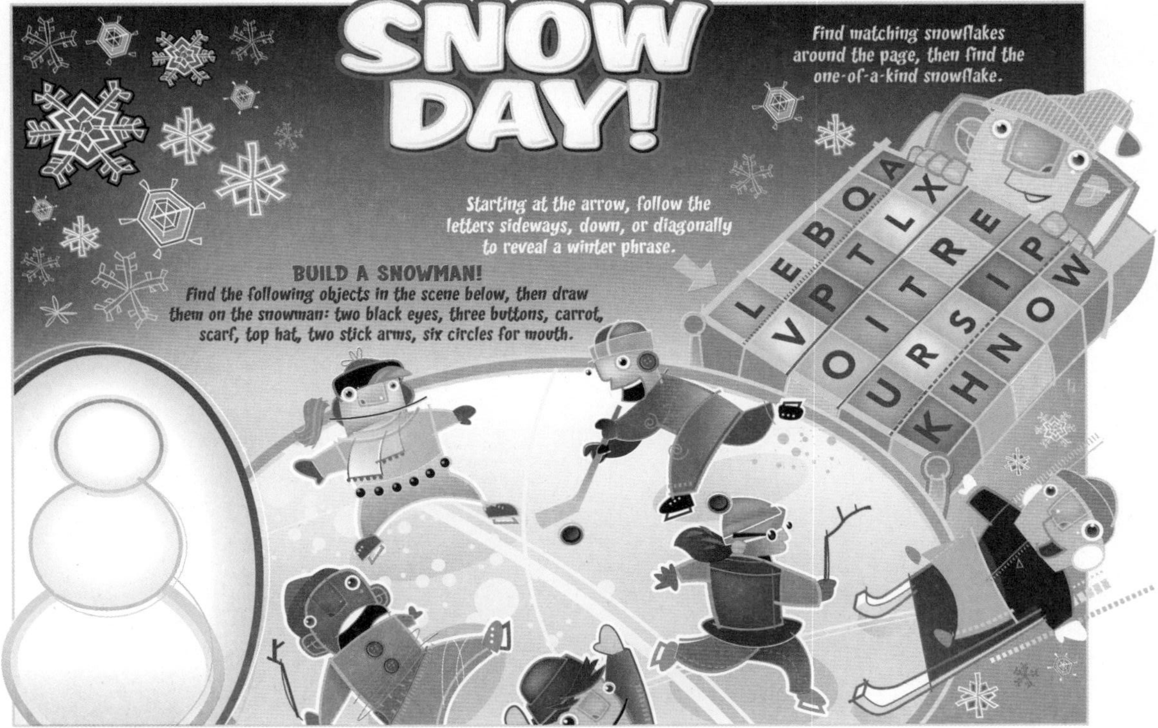

Answers on page 129.

Answers on page 130.

That Takes the Cake

Decorating this delicious doodle is cause for celebration. Use the decorative candies below for ideas, or come up with your own cake-decorating design. Decorate the remaining candies, too.

A DAY AT THE ZOO
HEY, THEY LEFT THE DOOR OPEN! LET'S GET TO THE BANANAS!
START
FINISH

Answers on page 130.

Dino Dots

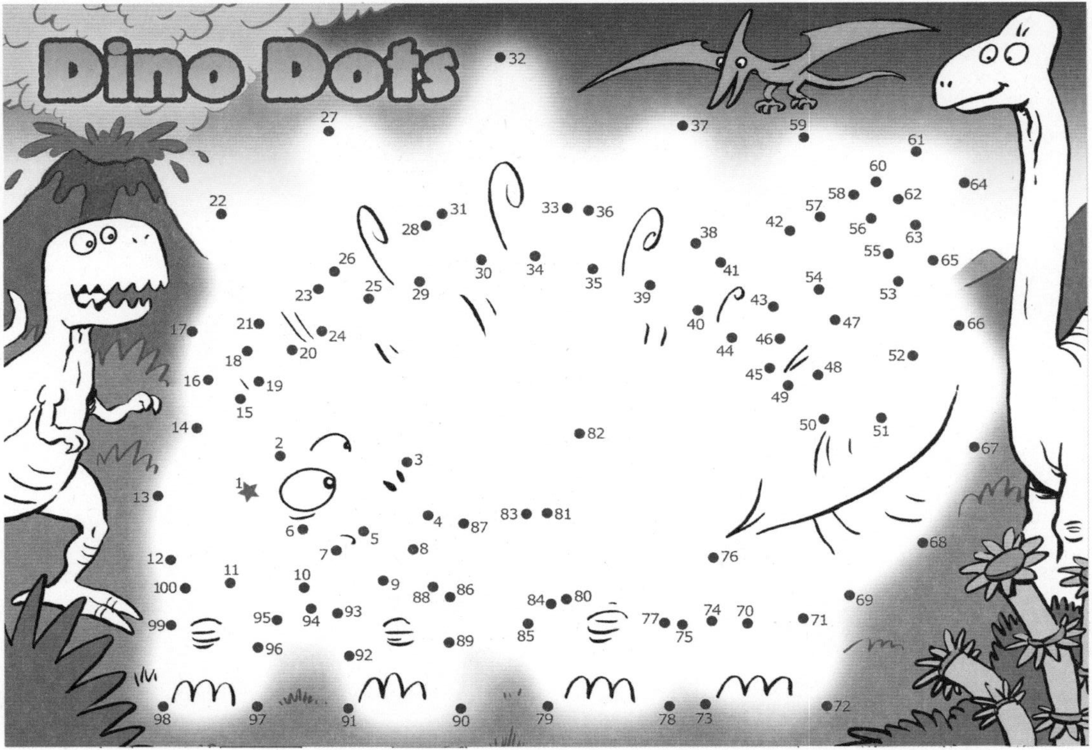

Answers on page 130.

Answers on page 130.

PUMPKIN PATCH
CHALLENGE
We found our pumpkins! Now help us get through the patch and the corn maze to the EXIT!
START
Sorry-GO BACK
Nope
CORN MAZE
Oops
EXIT

Answers on page 131.

Under the Sea
Find these objects in the crusty coral.
net
bubble
hook
worm
boat
Can you spot the five differences between these two sharks?
There are five pairs of matching fish. Can you spot them?
Help Gil the Guppy get home to his wife, Gillian.
START
FINISH

Answers on page 131.

Answers on page 131.

Got It Covered

READ THE TITLES OF THESE TWO BOOKS, THEN ILLUSTRATE WHAT YOU THINK THE COVERS SHOULD LOOK LIKE.

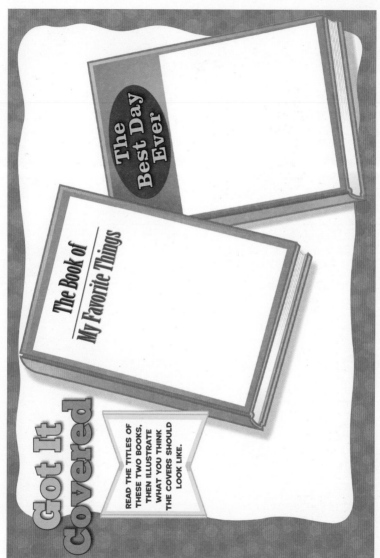

ON THE FARM
It's dinnertime!
Help Bessie back to the barn.
START
FINISH

Answers on page 131.

Answers on page 132.

GYM CLASS

Circle the matching set of tennis rackets.

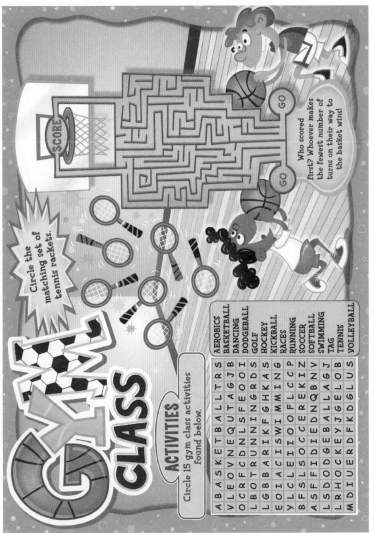

Who scored first? Whoever makes the fewest number of turns on their way to the basket wins!

ACTIVITIES

Circle 15 gym class activities found below.

A	B	A	S	K	E	T	B	A	L	L	T	R	S
V	L	E	O	V	N	E	Q	U	T	A	G	J	B
O	C	R	F	C	D	N	L	S	F	E	O	O	I
L	B	O	T	R	U	N	N	I	N	G	R	D	S
L	G	B	B	A	R	I	K	F	G	H	K	A	S
E	O	I	A	C	I	S	W	I	M	M	I	N	G
Y	L	C	L	E	I	I	O	O	F	L	C	C	P
B	F	S	L	S	O	C	C	E	R	E	K	I	Z
A	S	F	F	I	D	I	E	D	N	Q	B	N	V
L	S	D	O	D	G	E	B	A	L	L	A	G	J
L	R	H	O	C	K	E	Y	J	G	E	L	O	B
M	D	I	U	E	R	D	F	K	D	G	L	U	S

AEROBICS
BASKETBALL
DANCING
DODGEBALL
GOLF
HOCKEY
KICKBALL
RACES
RUNNING
SOCCER
SOFTBALL
SWIMMING
TAG
TENNIS
VOLLEYBALL

Answers on page 132.

PASTA-MANIA
Mama Mia, that's a lot of spaghetti!
Find your way from our hungry eater
to the spicy meatball at the end!
YUM!
FINISH

Answers on page 132.

Dinosaur Doodle

Draw this prehistoric pal in four easy steps. Give it other dinosaur friends, or create an entire Jurassic scene.

GOING UNDERGROUND

Answers on page 132.

Where's Charlie?
Oh, no! My hamster, Charlie, got out! Can you help me find him?
Start
Finish

Answers on page 133.

TREASURE HUNT

Start your quest for ancient riches by jumping from skull to skull! Each skull must have even-numbered teeth and be touching each other. **Be Brave!**

Whew! You made it to the treasure trove. There are seven matching pairs of treasure chests. Find them, cross them out, and the one chest remaining is the one filled with treasure. *Yahoo!*

Answers on page 133.

the water park

Follow the waterslides to find out which makes it to the end.

Use letters from the word below to make as many new words as possible:

SPLASHDOWN

WORD SEARCH

Find the following words:

backstroke, cannonball, diving, earplugs, goggles, innertube, summer, sunscreen, swimsuit

N	W	V	C	E	K	O	R	T	S	K	C	A	B	T
Y	U	Z	D	Q	Q	U	G	U	M	T	W	Q	D	I
Z	G	H	S	B	L	U	B	O	Q	G	H	H	I	U
W	W	N	O	N	A	A	O	K	G	A	H	B	V	S
C	A	N	N	O	N	B	A	L	L	G	G	L	I	M
E	B	U	T	R	E	N	N	I	G	O	L	W	N	I
U	S	U	N	S	C	R	E	E	N	B	Y	E	G	W
E	A	R	P	L	U	G	S	R	E	M	M	U	S	S

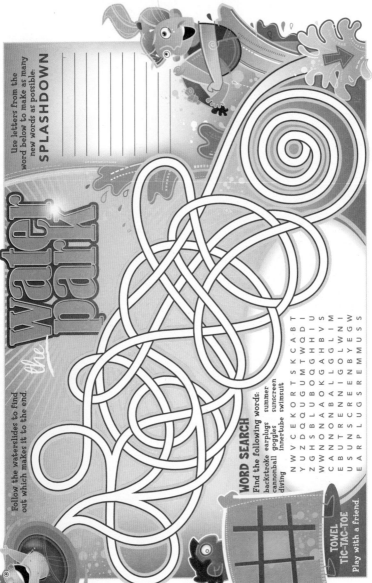

TOWEL TIC-TAC-TOE

Play with a friend.

Answers on page 133.

Map for Mexico
Aside from the many beaches, deserts, and mountains, Mexico is also known for its jungles. Unscramble the letters to spell out some animals that can be found in Mexico.
RODIECLOC
RUJAAG
RATPOR
KOMYEN
Can you name the four states that border Mexico?
MEXICAN SUDOKU
ACROSS
2. Decorated container filled with candy
3. Favorite sport in Mexico
4. Mexico's capital
DOWN
1. Flatbread made of corn or flour
2. Mexican dollar
5. Vegetable used to make nachos
1
2
3
4
5
Did you know chocolate was invented in Mexico? What are your favorite chocolate dishes?
MEXICO
PACIFIC OCEAN
MEXICO CITY

Answers on page 133.

Answers on page 134.

MIX & MATCH FACE

USE THE FACIAL FEATURES SHOWN TO CREATE AN INTERESTING CHARACTER ON THIS BLANK FACE. TOP OFF YOUR DRAWING WITH THE SUGGESTED HATS OR HAIRPIECES.

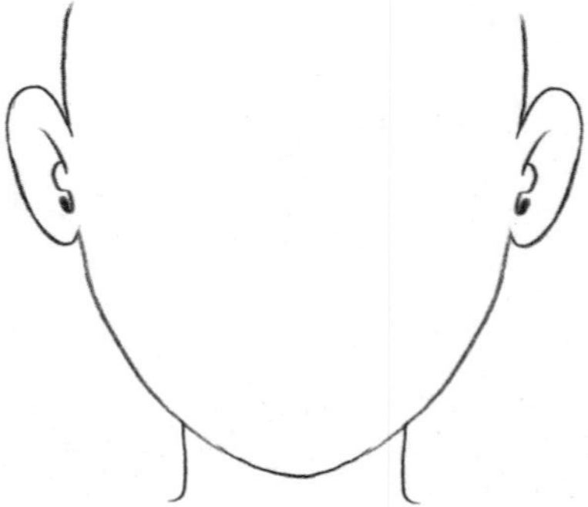

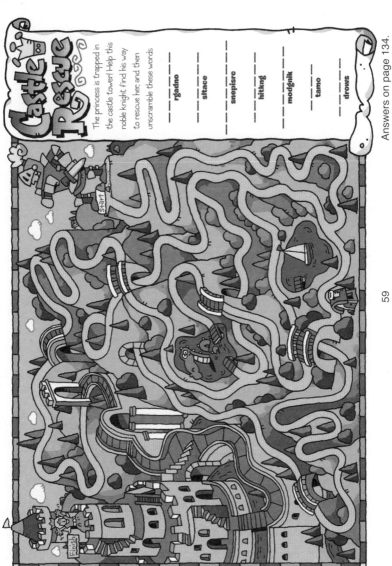

Castle Rescue

The princess is trapped in the castle tower! Help this noble knight find his way to rescue her, and then unscramble these words.

__ __ __ __ __ __
rgadno

__ __ __ __ __ __
sltace

__ __ __ __ __ __ __ __
snepisrc

__ __ __ __ __ __
hitkng

__ __ __ __ __ __ __
modgnik

__ __ __ __
tamo

__ __ __ __ __
drows

Answers on page 134.

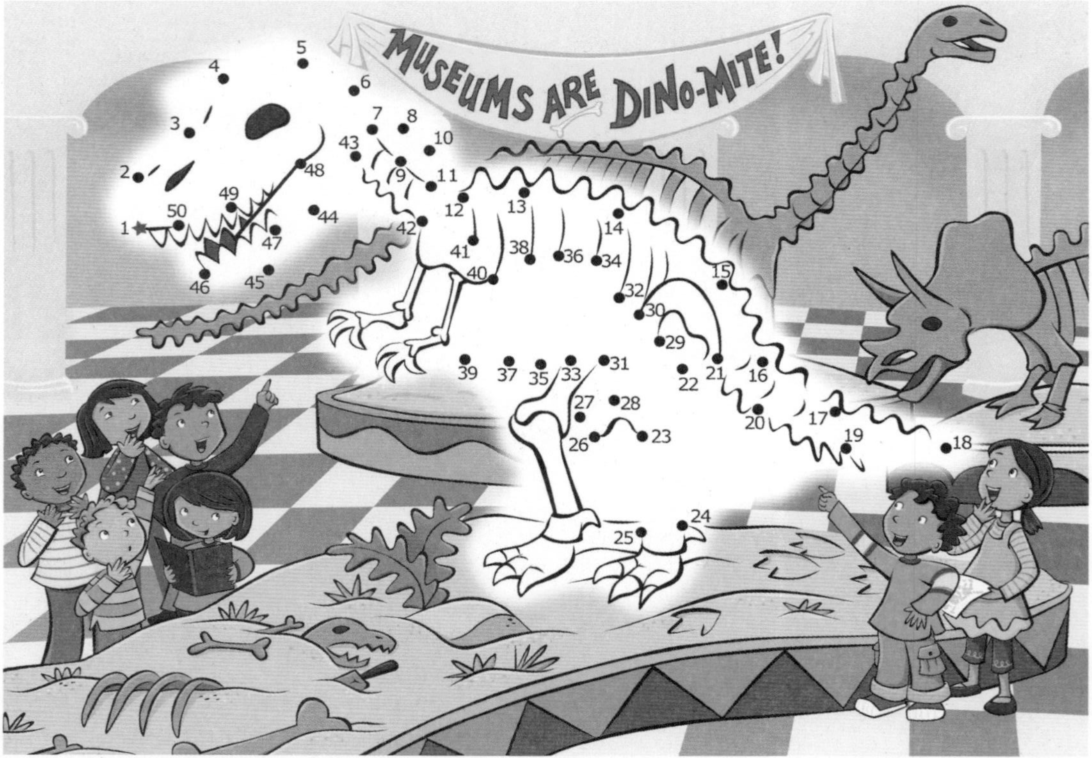
MUSEUMS ARE DINO-MITE!

Answers on page 134.

JUNGLE EXPLORATION
CAN YOU HELP THE MIGHTY JUNGLE MAN GET HOME SO HE CAN ENJOY A DELICIOUS BANANA SHAKE?!!
SNAKES!
PIRANHAS!
GULP!
MMM - DELICIOUS BANANA SHAKE!

Answers on page 134.

Rover's Lost!

Oh, no! Rover has wandered off again, and he can't remember how to get back. Help him find his way home for dinner. Then solve these word puzzles.

1. 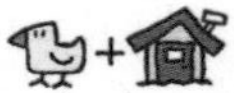

______

2. 

______

3. 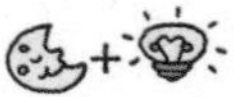

______

4. 

______

Answers on page 135.

Mini Golf
There's only one path that leads to the hole. Which one is it, 1, 2, or 3? Help the player find the right one!
1
2
3

Answers on page 135.

Pirates!!
There are 10 bones hidden in the picture. Find them or walk the plank!
Aaargh Matey! Copy the pictures in each numbered square into the same numbered square in the grid.
There are 20 things in this picture that start with a "p". Can you find them?
A2
C1
B3
B1
C3
A3
A1
C2
B2
A
B
C
1
2
3
zzzzz

Answers on page 135.

Going Bananas

Finish the rest of this gorilla, using the first half as a guide.

Answers on page 135.

QUEST for FUEL
ZOOB IS RUNNING OUT OF FUEL!
HELP HIM FIND THE WAY TO THE STATION.
START
FINISH
FUEL

Answers on page 136.

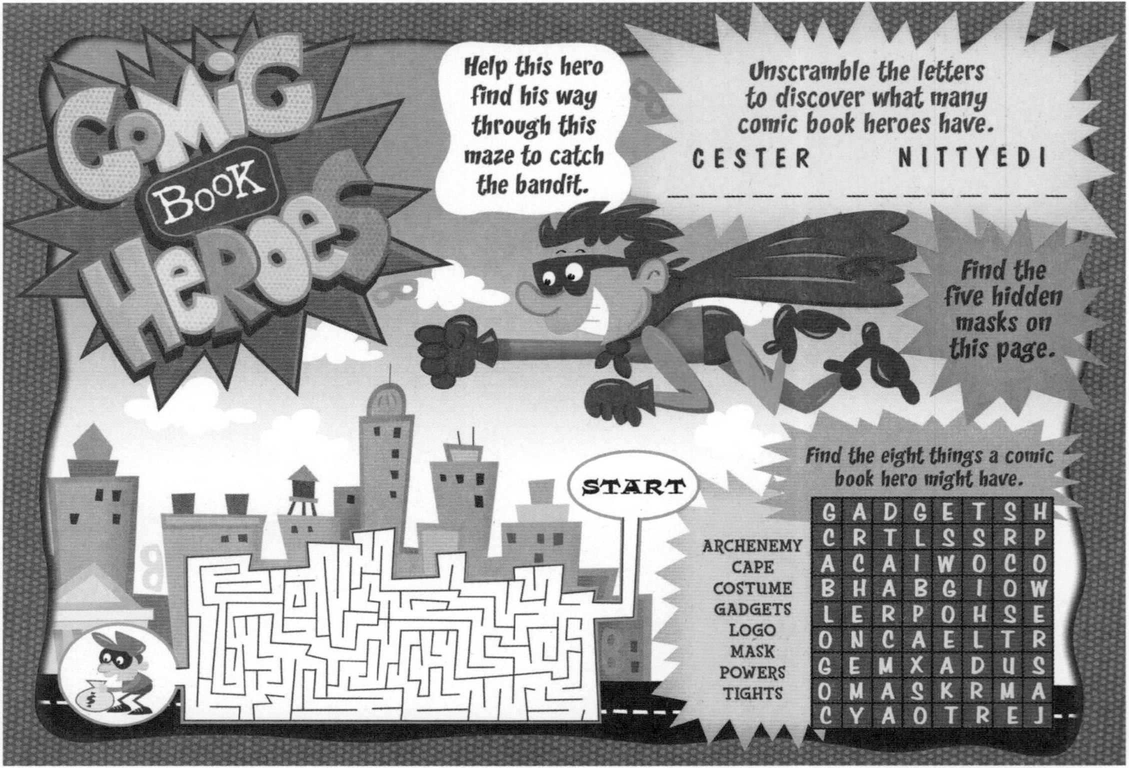
Comic Book Heroes
Help this hero find his way through this maze to catch the bandit.
Unscramble the letters to discover what many comic book heroes have.
CESTER NITTYEDI
Find the five hidden masks on this page.
START
Find the eight things a comic book hero might have.
ARCHENEMY
CAPE
COSTUME
GADGETS
LOGO
MASK
POWERS
TIGHTS
G A D G E T S H
C R T L S S R P
A C A I W O C O
B H A B G I O W
L E R P O H S E
O N C A E L T R
G E M X A D U S
O M A S K R M A
C Y A O T R E J

Answers on page 136.

ANTARCTICA ADVENTURE
Help Ziggy cross the floating ice so he can get to his mom.
START
END
Unscramble the letters below to find out what it's like in Antarctica.
FEZINEGR DOLC

Answers on page 136.

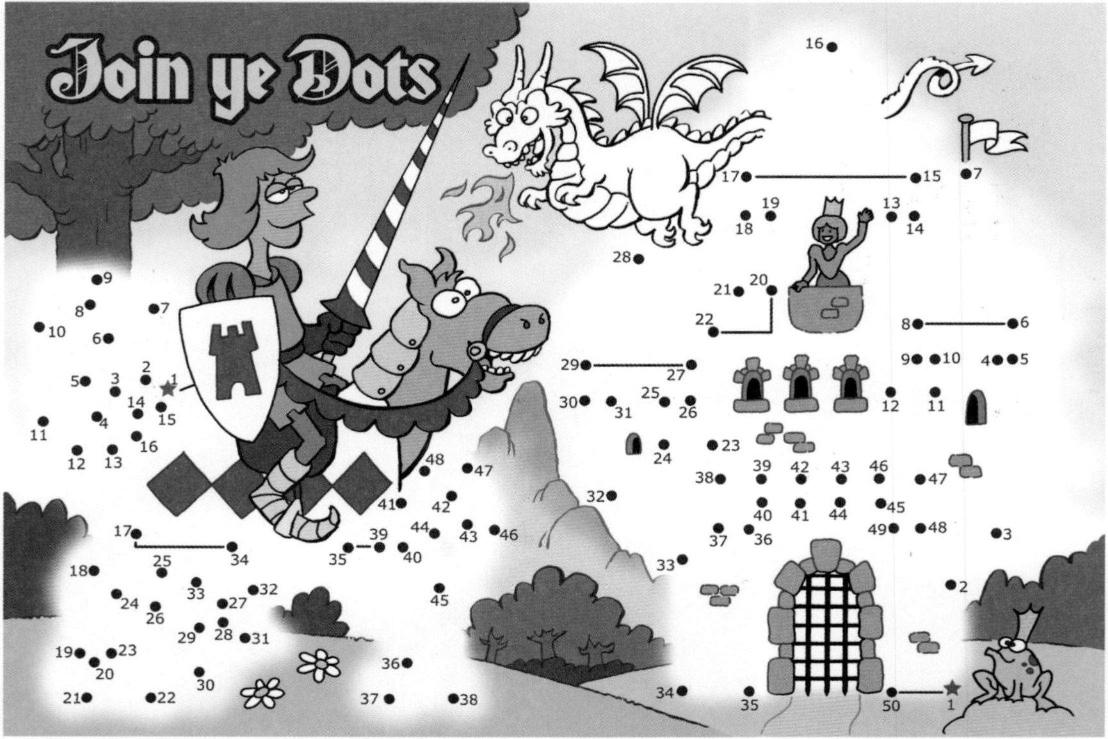

Answers on page 136.

Last Night I Dreamt...
WHAT'S THE CRAZIEST DREAM YOU'VE EVER HAD? OR, WHEN YOU LIE IN BED AT NIGHT, WHAT DO YOU THINK ABOUT? WHATEVER YOUR DREAMS, DOODLE THEM HERE!

School Map

This new student needs to get to the cafeteria, but first he has to stop in the math, science, and history rooms in that order. Use the School Map to help him find his way!

B	D	O	G	B	N	E	G
X	F	M	V	S	D	S	B
H	C	N	U	L	S	W	O
E	A	T	H	I	U	J	O
A	S	R	E	C	Z	A	K
D	C	R	A	N	B	C	S
L	T	O	B	E	A	T	E
N	R	E	D	P	S	E	S
O	O	B	K	Z	C	M	N
T	T	C	A	T	I	O	T
E	A	M	O	P	S	E	O
B	L	E	R	A	S	E	R
O	U	H	E	Y	O	S	U
O	C	N	I	A	R	T	L
K	L	L	N	B	S	U	E
P	A	P	E	R	C	L	R
W	C	L	I	P	S	O	N

WORD SEARCH

BACKPACK, BOOKS, CALCULATOR, ERASER, LUNCH, NOTEBOOK, PAPER, PENCILS, RULER, SCISSORS

Answers on page 137.

Monster Bash

Find all of the words in the list in the letters at the bottom.

GROSS-ERY LIST
- broccoli
- hairballs
- newt
- sardines
- toadstool
- toenails
- warts

```
Y R I A X L E G N T N O
H S A R D I N E S D D M
M N H I Y H R E N Q R V
T M S G J A F P W A W R
B V N R K O P Q C T T P
Y X C U I T O N B J R N
T L Y L O O T S D A O T
D E P S N G W F L A D E
T O E N A I L S X S D J
S Y I L O C C O R B O Y
S H A I R B A L L S A I
Z S T R A W G R Y T B T
```

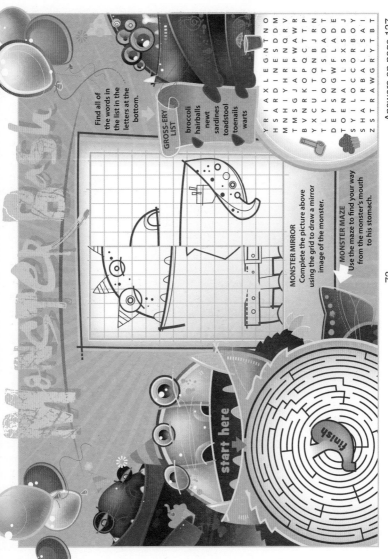

MONSTER MIRROR
Complete the picture above using the grid to draw a mirror image of the monster.

MONSTER MAZE
Use the maze to find your way from the monster's mouth to his stomach.

start here

finish

Answers on page 137.

Answers on page 137.

WHO'S GOT THE FISH?
Here fishy, fishy!
Who was lucky enough to catch a fish?
NICE CATCH!
Dad is lucky! Connect the dots from 1 to 33 and then color in his catch.
GONE FISHIN'
THE OUTSIDER
Find the one that doesn't fit among the others and circle it!
COUNT 'EM ALL!
Mom is checking to be sure she has all her babies. Help her count them. Then circle the number that shows the correct amount.
53
56
58

Answers on page 137.

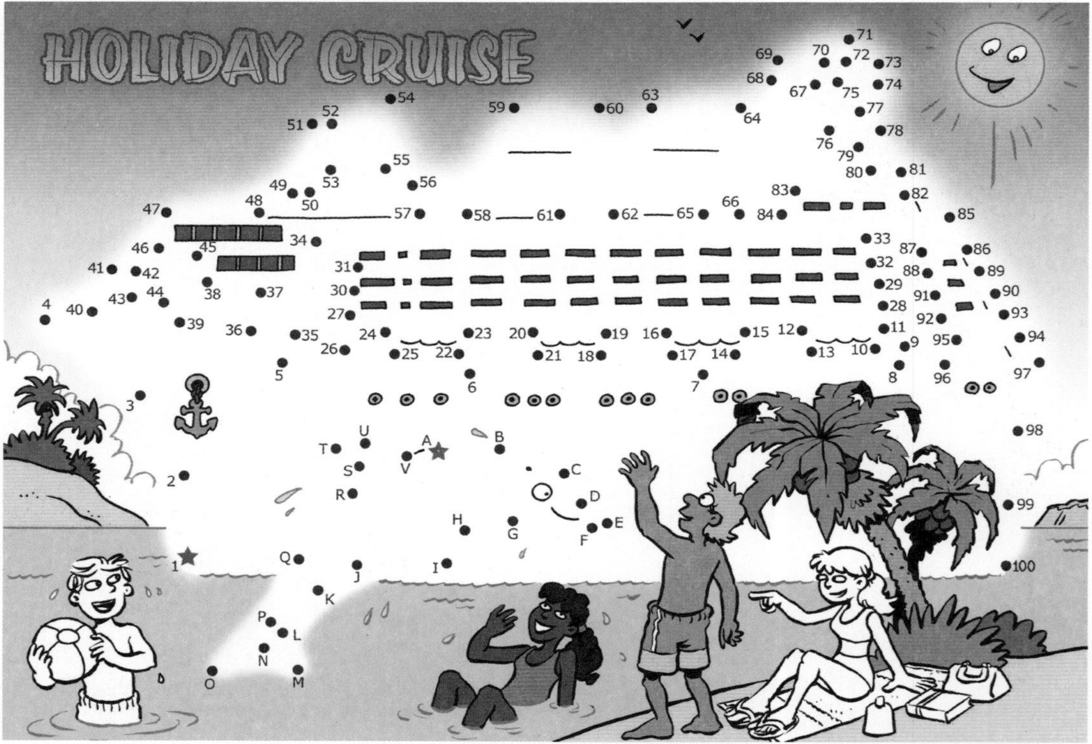

Answers on page 138.

ROYAL DRAWINGS
This king and queen do not look as regal as they should.
Give them fancy clothes and crowns so they are ready for the next royal gathering.

Robots!

Follow the circuit board maze to the center.

Match the correct tool below with the shapes on the robot.

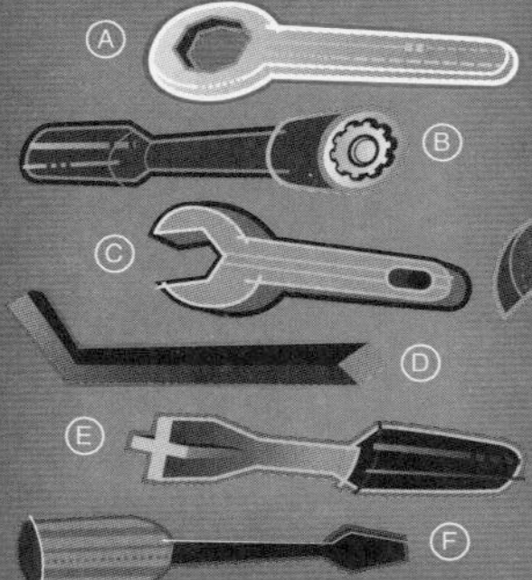

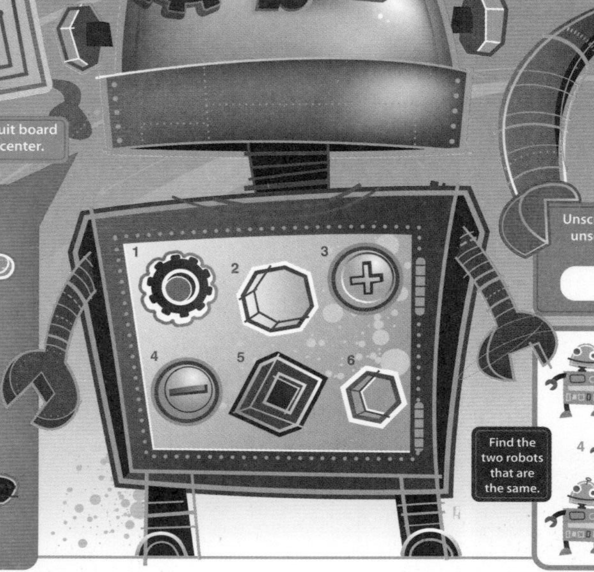

R E (P) W O

(M) A P G O R R

C E L T R I (C) E

C (O) R N L O T

(T) H I S W C

W I S (E) R

L O (U) D P A

O B O E (R) T

Unscramble the words above, then unscramble the circled letters to decode the secret word:

Find the two robots that are the same.

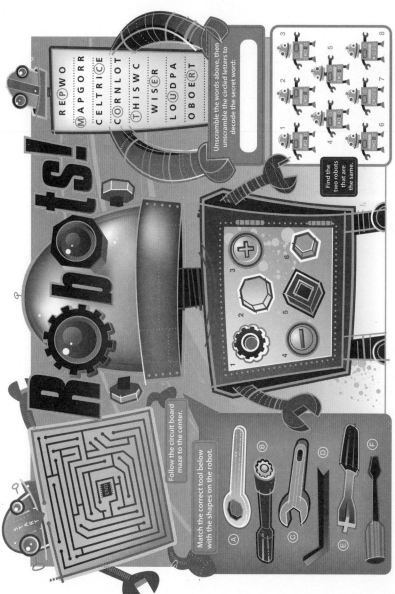

Answers on page 138.

DOWNHILL RUN

Answers on page 138.

Create a Masterpiece

The *Mona Lisa*'s got nothing on your doodles! Draw pieces of art in the frames for display in this art gallery.

Get to Gramma's House!

Little Red Riding Hood is on her way to Gramma's House with dinner. Help Red find her way through the woods. Then use the code below to see what she brought in her basket for dinner!

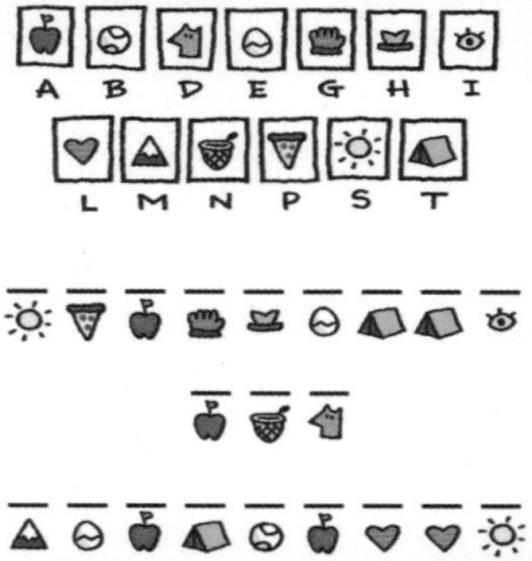

Answers on page 138.

ELEPHANT FUN

Draw this elephant in five easy steps.

Growing Green

Circle the 12 trees.

APPLE	DOGWOOD	MAPLE
ASH	ELDER	OAK
ASPEN	ELM	PINE
BIRCH	LILAC	PLUM

The uncircled letters in order tell what you need to grow trees.

S	D	U	A	S	P	E	N
M	N	O	A	P	L	U	M
A	S	H	G	N	P	E	D
P	I	N	E	W	R	L	A
L	I	L	A	C	O	M	E
E	L	D	E	R	A	O	I
B	I	R	C	H	K	N	D

Circle the matching watering cans.

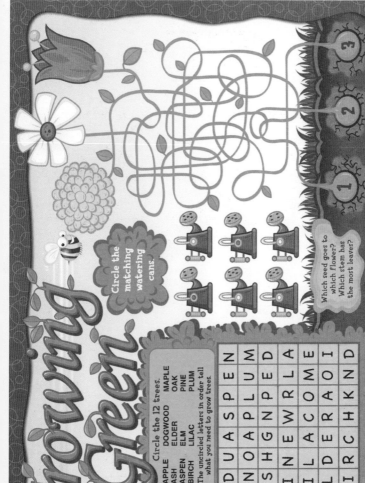

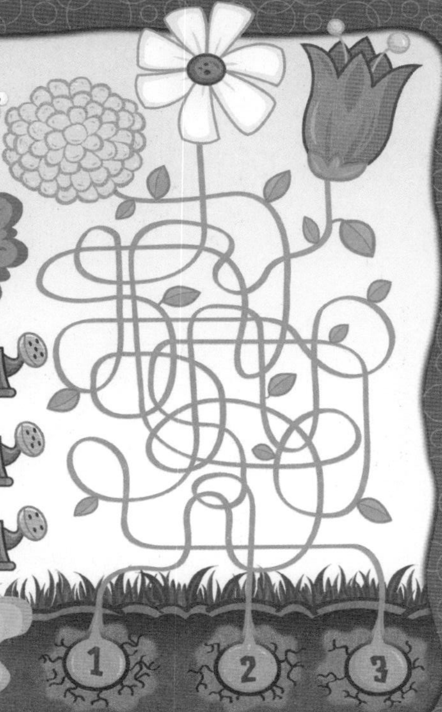

Which seed goes to which flower? Which stem has the most leaves?

Answers on page 139.

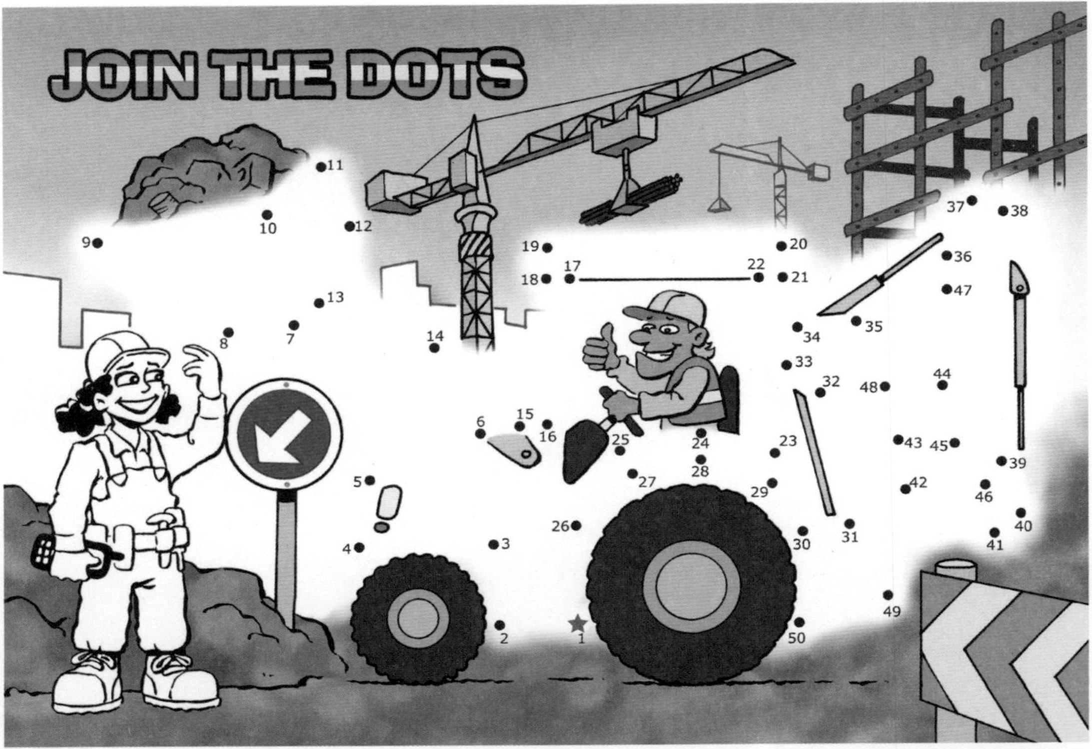
JOIN THE DOTS

Answers on page 139.

Fishy Friends
Help the angelfish find his friends.
START
zzz
FINISH

Answers on page 139.

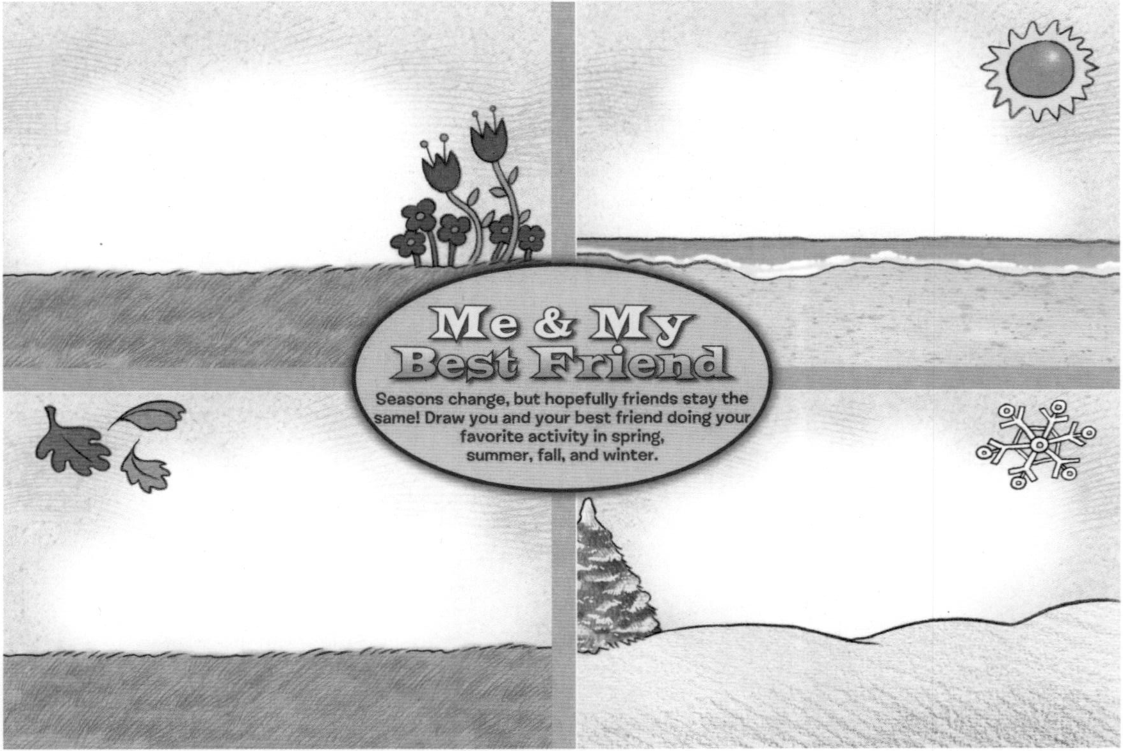

Me & My Best Friend

Seasons change, but hopefully friends stay the same! Draw you and your best friend doing your favorite activity in spring, summer, fall, and winter.

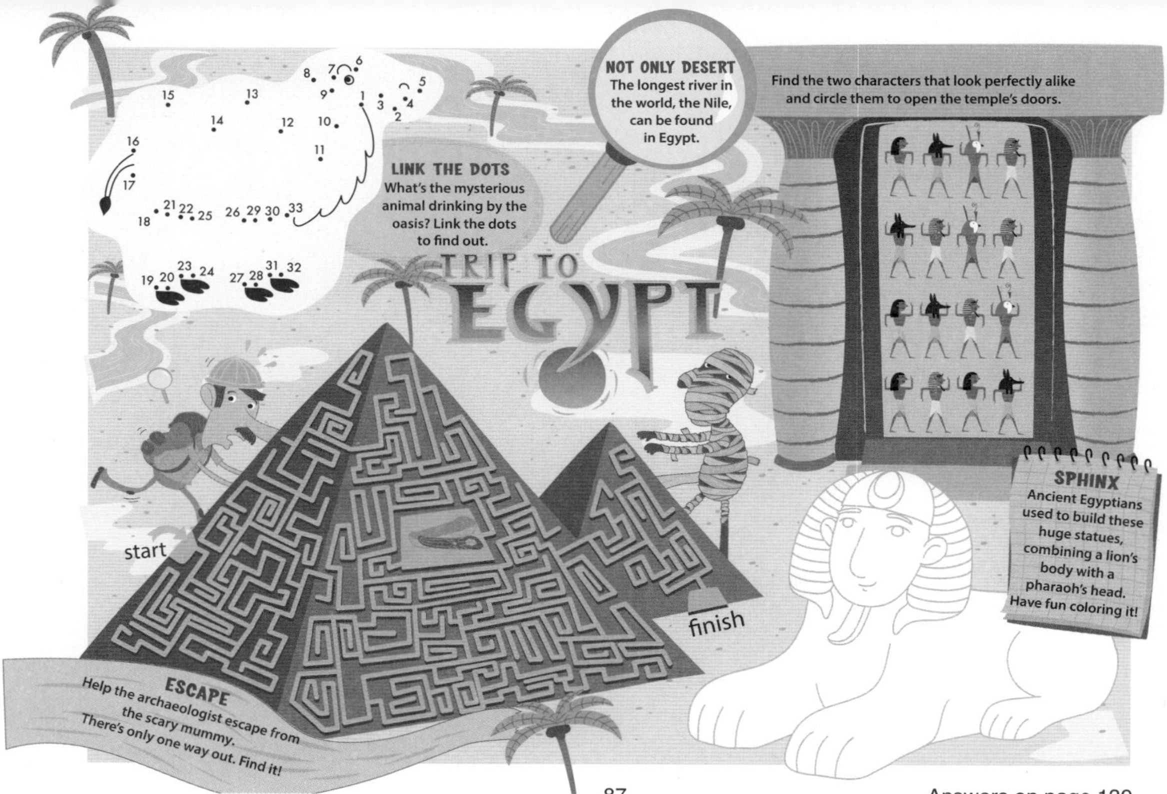

TRIP TO EGYPT
NOT ONLY DESERT
The longest river in the world, the Nile, can be found in Egypt.
Find the two characters that look perfectly alike and circle them to open the temple's doors.
LINK THE DOTS
What's the mysterious animal drinking by the oasis? Link the dots to find out.
start
finish
ESCAPE
Help the archaeologist escape from the scary mummy. There's only one way out. Find it!
SPHINX
Ancient Egyptians used to build these huge statues, combining a lion's body with a pharaoh's head. Have fun coloring it!

Answers on page 139.

Sightseeing in Paris

Answers on page 140.

STYLIZED SIGNATURE

Copy this fun and funky lettering — or come up with your own letter designs — to write your name in some new and unique ways.

abcdef
ghijklmn
opqrst
uvwxyz

ABCD
EFGHI
JKLM
NOPQ
RSTUV
WXYZ

abcde
fghijkl
mnopq
rs+uv
wxyz

a b c d e f
g h i j k
l m n o p
q r s t u
v w x y z

EVEREST
CHALLENGE
HELP THESE CLIMBERS TO THE TOP OF THE WORLD! BE SURE TO STOP AT EACH CAMPSITE ALONG THE WAY.
Mt. Everest
GO BACK
A
B
C
Start

Watch Your Step!
Climbing BONUS
ONLY SIX ROCKS ON THIS CLIMB HAVE NUMBERS THAT DON'T TOUCH A ROCK WITH THE SAME NUMBER. CAN YOU FIND THEM?

Answers on page 140.

CITY LIFE

Turn this empty space into a bustling city filled with buildings, storefronts, people, and more.

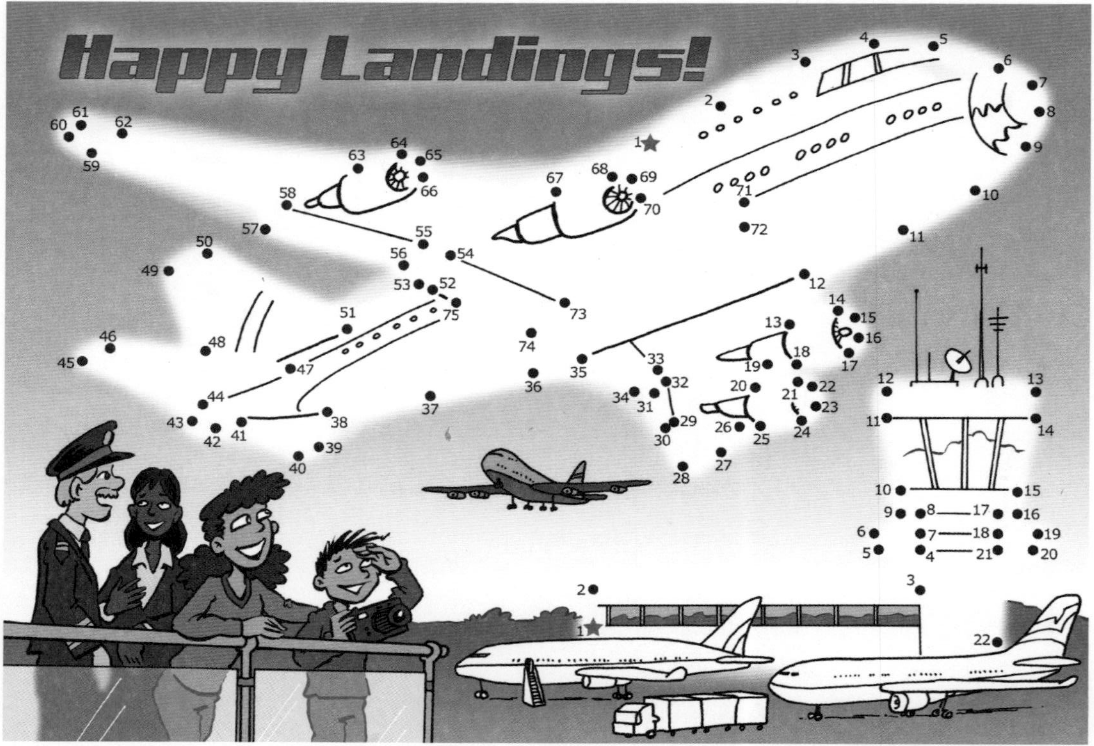

Answers on page 140.

Across the U.S.A.
Hint: Which city is called "The Windy City"?
Unscramble the letters below to spell out the names of seven states.
OLDACORO
TUAH
ARILFOD
AGIMCHIN
SATEX
GERNOO
NORAZIA
Which two states do not touch any other states?
Which state is the "Sunshine State"?
Which city is called "The Big Apple"?

Answers on page 140.

ANIMAL MATCHUP
Doodle the animal that likes to eat — or at least gnaw on — each object shown. For example, a dog likes to chew on a bone.

Winter Wear

Warm up this family of snowpeople with hats, scarves, gloves, boots – you name it! Then add facial features and other details to complete the cool look.

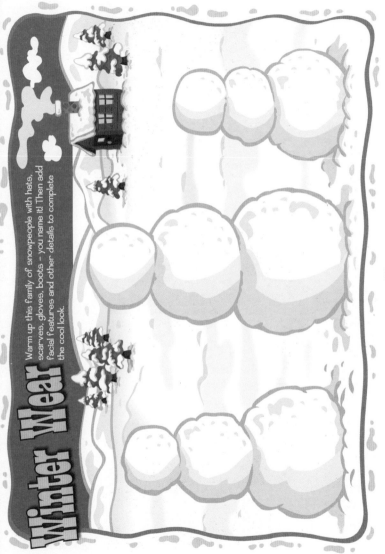

Ride 'em Cowboy!

Answers on page 141.

Top It Off

A big hat or funny hair? Or both? Be creative and finish the "tops" of these characters.

DAY AT THE BALLGAME

SCORE A SNACK!

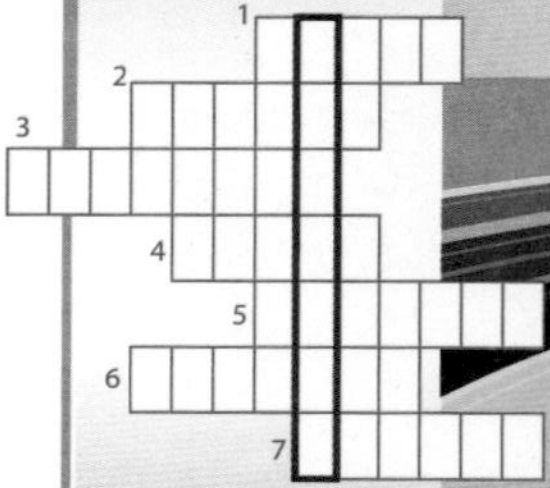

Fill in the spaces above with the names of the snacks below. Then read the secret phrase in the middle.

Find 12 objects that don't belong on the ballfield.

Fill in the blanks to spell the names of baseball teams. Then unscramble the circled letters and fill in the umpire's phrase.

C◯R __ I __ A◯S

M __ R◯I __ S

◯H __ L◯I __ S

◯R __ V __ S

◯A __ K __ E __

R◯N __ E __ S

Answers on page 141.

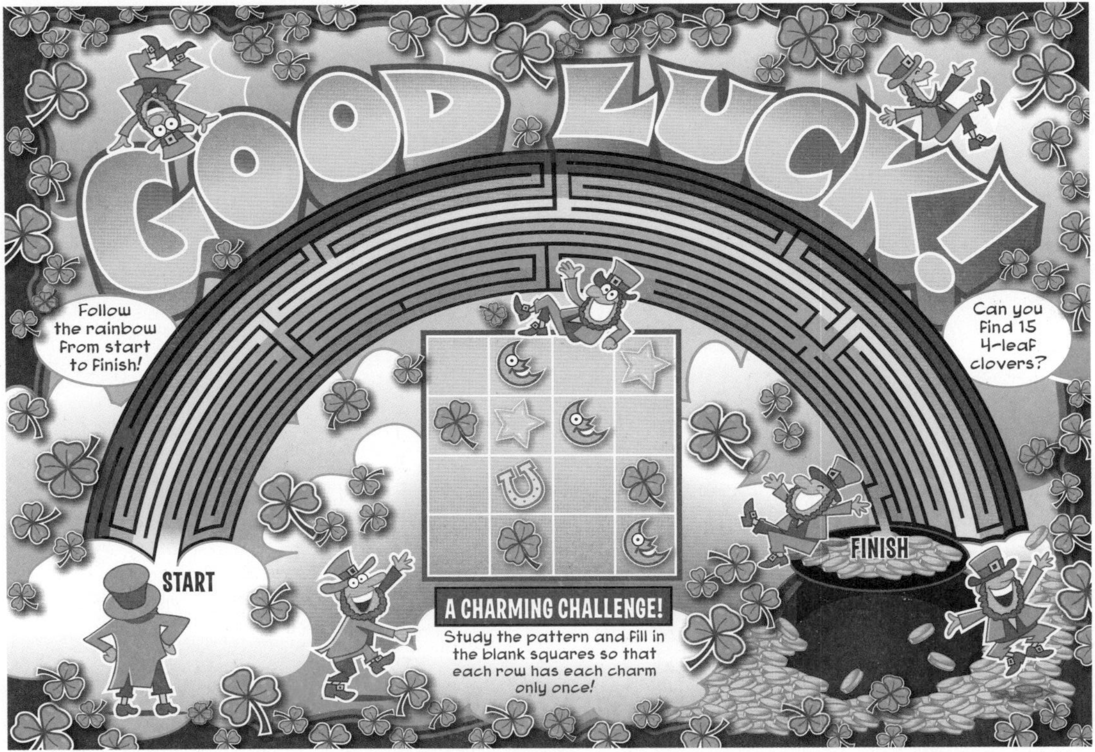
GOOD LUCK!
Follow the rainbow from start to finish!
Can you find 15 4-leaf clovers?
START
FINISH
A CHARMING CHALLENGE!
Study the pattern and fill in the blank squares so that each row has each charm only once!

Answers on page 141.

AFRICAN SAVANNA

Can you spot the seven differences between the mirror images of these animals?

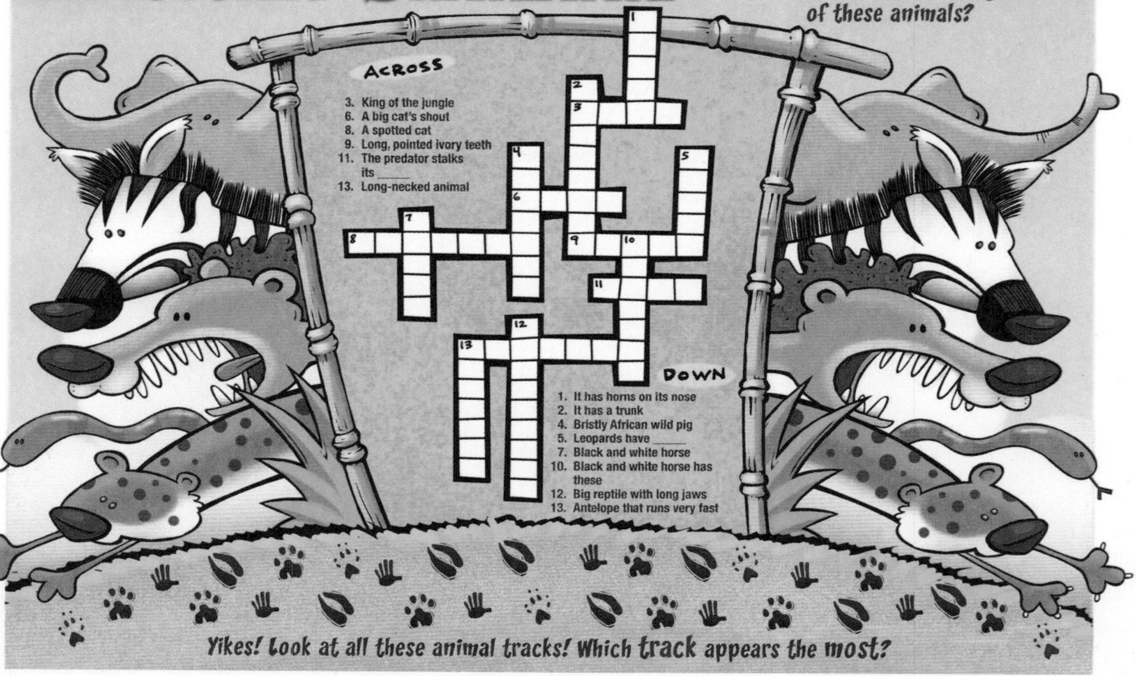

ACROSS

3. King of the jungle
6. A big cat's shout
8. A spotted cat
9. Long, pointed ivory teeth
11. The predator stalks its ____
13. Long-necked animal

DOWN

1. It has horns on its nose
2. It has a trunk
4. Bristly African wild pig
5. Leopards have ____
7. Black and white horse
10. Black and white horse has these
12. Big reptile with long jaws
13. Antelope that runs very fast

Yikes! Look at all these animal tracks! Which track appears the most?

Answers on page 141.

UP AND AWAY

Draw unique, colorful patterns in each hot air balloon. The sky's the limit with these doodles!

Answers on page 142.

GOING BUGGY!
WHICH SHADOW DOESN'T MATCH ITS ANT?
START!
HER MAJESTY NEEDS HELP! THIS POOR ANT QUEEN HAS BEEN WORKING THE NURSERY ALL DAY, AND SHE'S HUNGRY! HELP THE WORKER ANTS GET FOOD TO THEIR QUEEN.
STOP! IN ORDER TO CONTINUE, FIRST DECIPHER THESE CODES:
+
+ R + - O + R
- Tash + +

Answers on page 142.

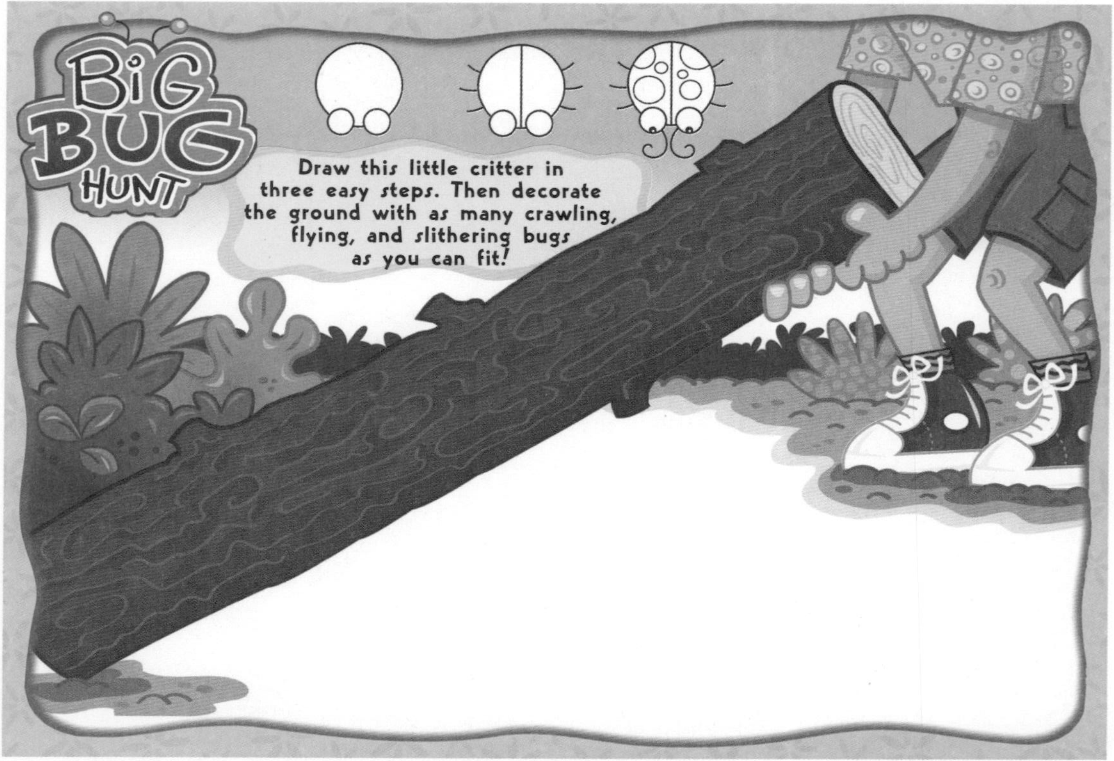
BIG BUG HUNT
Draw this little critter in three easy steps. Then decorate the ground with as many crawling, flying, and slithering bugs as you can fit!

TRAIN TRIP

CHOO CHOO CHOOSE
Only one of the shadows below matches the little train perfectly. Which one is it?

THE RIGHT TRACK
Looks like the engineer needs some help! Find the way to the tunnel.

FIND THE DIFFERENCES
The two scenes are similar, but the second one has 10 differences. Circle them all!

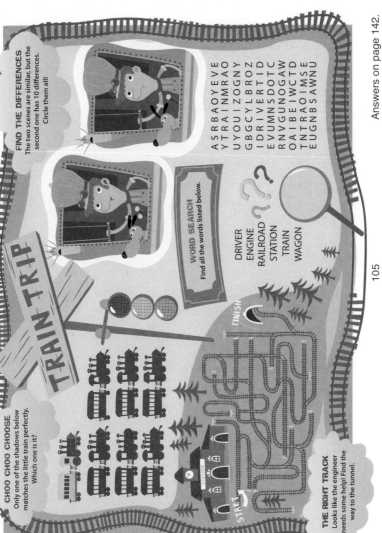

WORD SEARCH
Find all the words listed below.

DRIVER
ENGINE
RAILROAD
STATION
TRAIN
WAGON

A	S	R	B	A	O	Y	E	V	E
Y	T	R	A	I	N	M	R	A	O
U	Y	O	U	I	Z	O	G	N	Y
G	B	G	C	Y	L	B	R	O	Z
I	D	R	I	V	E	R	T	I	D
E	V	U	M	N	S	D	O	T	C
R	N	V	G	U	N	O	G	A	W
O	A	I	B	E	I	W	C	T	D
T	N	T	R	A	O	I	M	S	E
E	U	G	N	B	S	A	W	N	U

Answers on page 142.

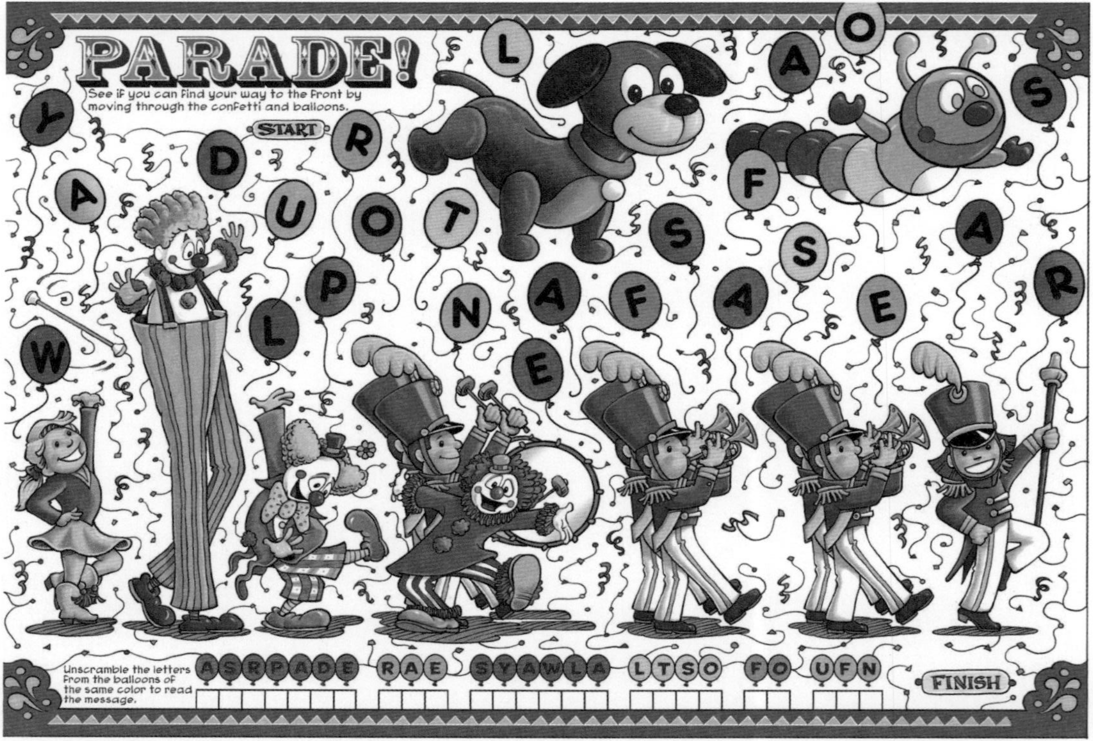
PARADE!
See if you can find your way to the front by moving through the confetti and balloons.
START
Y
A
W
D
U
L
P
R
O
T
N
E
A
F
S
L
A
O
F
S
A
E
S
A
R
Unscramble the letters from the balloons of the same color to read the message.
ASRPADE RAE SYAWLA LTSO FO UFN
FINISH

Answers on page 142.

Putting on a
SHOW
The spotlight is on! Draw yourself dancing, acting, singing – whatever your talent – on this stage.

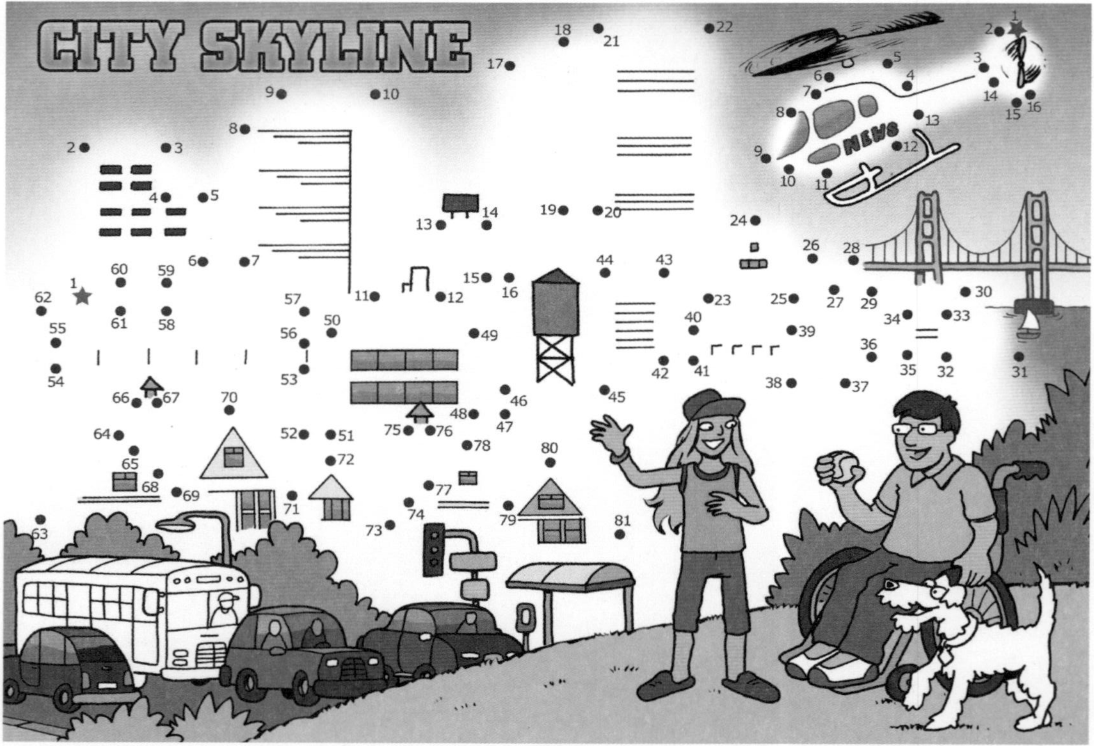

Answers on page 143.

MY ROOM

Transform this plain space into the room of your dreams.

What Happens Next?

Tell the story of this vacationing family by doodling the rest of this comic strip.

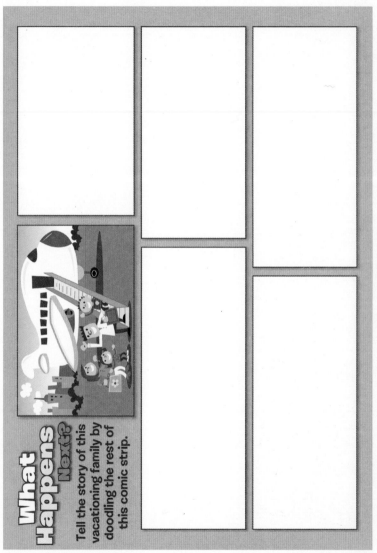

Mermaid Tails
These two mermaids are feeling a little incomplete. Finish drawing their bottom and top halves so they can swim free!

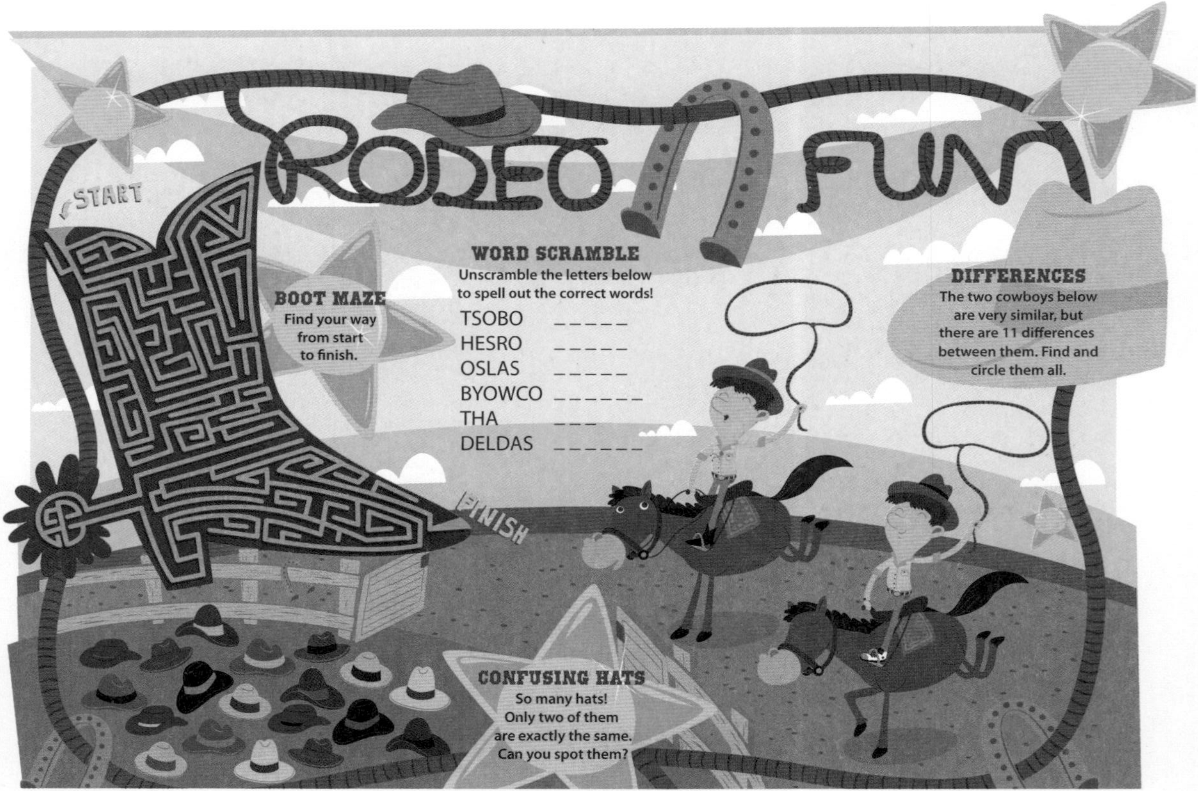
RODEO FUN
START
FINISH
BOOT MAZE
Find your way from start to finish.
WORD SCRAMBLE
Unscramble the letters below to spell out the correct words!
TSOBO _ _ _ _ _
HESRO _ _ _ _ _
OSLAS _ _ _ _ _
BYOWCO _ _ _ _ _ _
THA _ _ _
DELDAS _ _ _ _ _ _
DIFFERENCES
The two cowboys below are very similar, but there are 11 differences between them. Find and circle them all.
CONFUSING HATS
So many hats! Only two of them are exactly the same. Can you spot them?

Answers on page 143.

ALL ABOARD!

Draw this train engine in five steps as it pulls into the station.
Add train cars for even more doodle fun.

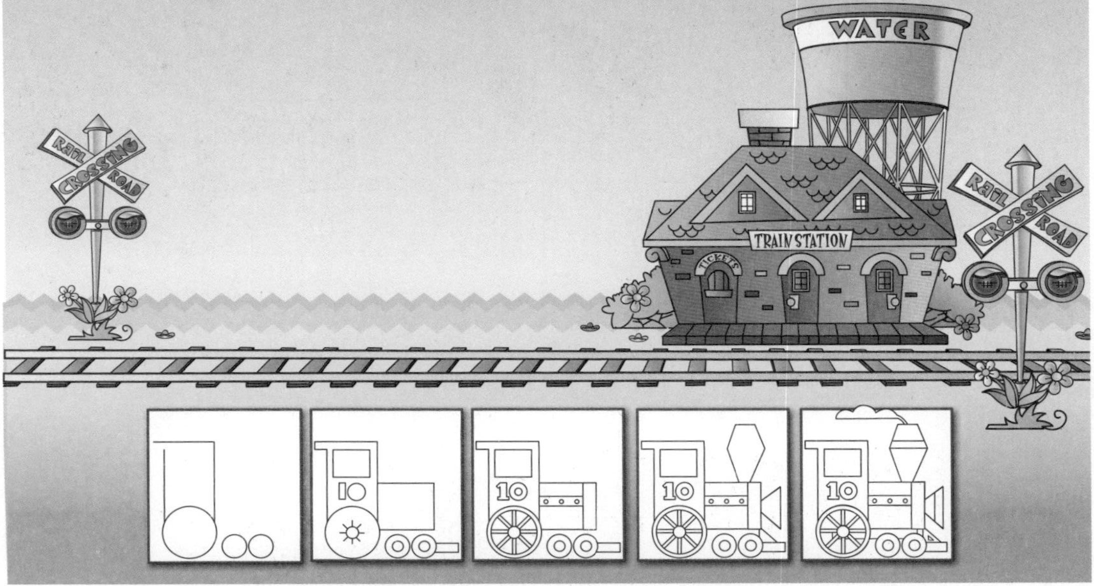

Answers on page 143.

The Big Game
WHO ARE ALL THESE PEOPLE CHEERING FOR? DRAW THE ACTION ON THE SPORTS FIELD, THEN FILL THE BLEACHERS WITH EVEN MORE FANS.

Answers on page 143.

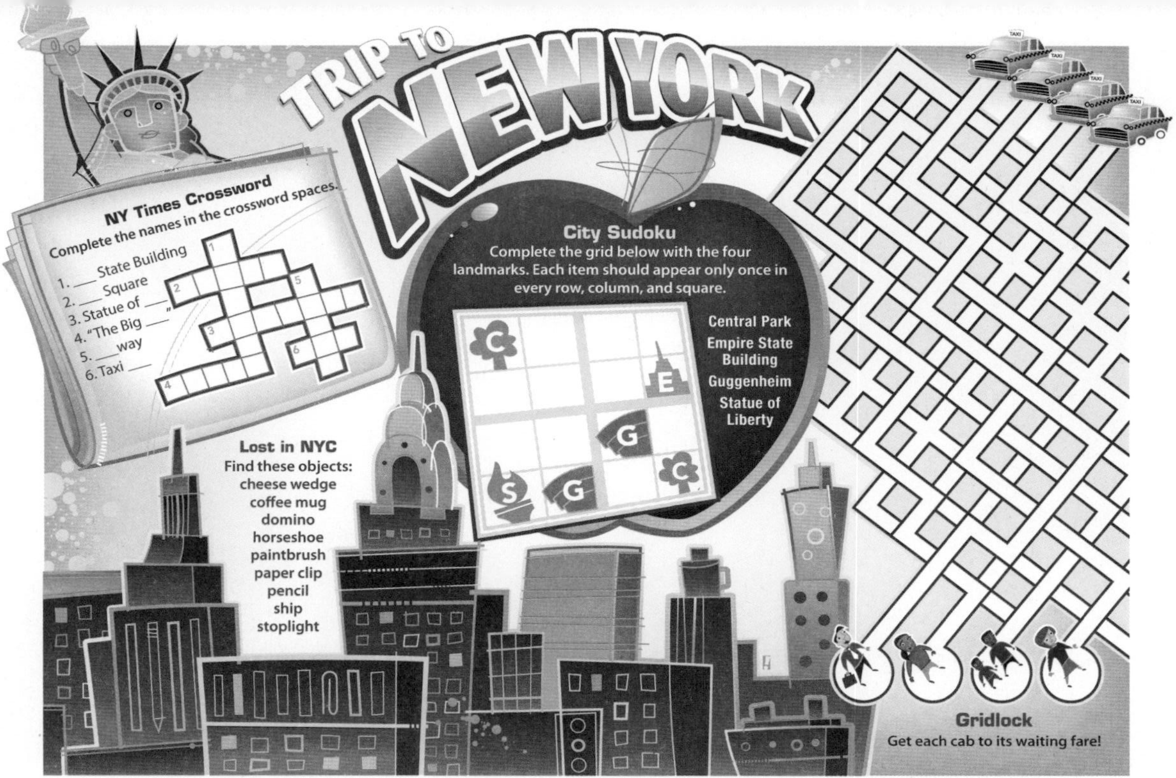
TRIP TO NEW YORK
NY Times Crossword
Complete the names in the crossword spaces.
1. ___ State Building
2. ___ Square
3. Statue of ___
4. "The Big ___"
5. ___way
6. Taxi ___
City Sudoku
Complete the grid below with the four landmarks. Each item should appear only once in every row, column, and square.
Central Park
Empire State Building
Guggenheim
Statue of Liberty
Lost in NYC
Find these objects:
cheese wedge
coffee mug
domino
horseshoe
paintbrush
paper clip
pencil
ship
stoplight
Gridlock
Get each cab to its waiting fare!

Answers on page 144.

Be a Hero!

If you could have superpowers, what would they be? Draw yourself in all your superhero glory below.

Visit The
Museum Maze
Welcome to the Museum!
Find your way from the entrance to the exit, but be sure to visit the Dinosaurs, Art, Heart, Egypt, Space, Automobiles, and Sculpture exhibits, then the Museum Gift Shop – in that order – before you leave!
SCULPTURE
The Bear
ART
SPACE
DINOSAURS
GIFTS
MUSEUM
EXIT
ENTER
HEART
Thump Thump
EGYPT
AUTOMOBILES
MUSEUM

Answers on page 144.

Answers on page 144.

ROYAL RESIDENCE

Add more stories, wings, details – you name it! – to create a castle fit for a king.

My DREAM HOME
WHAT KIND OF HOME DO YOU SEE YOURSELF LIVING IN SOMEDAY? A TRADITIONAL TWO-STORY HOUSE? A MODERN ECO-FRIENDLY SHELTER? USE THIS SPACE TO MAP OUTA BLUEPRINT FOR YOUR DREAM DWELLING.

ANSWERS

Wild and Wacky Waterslide (page 4)

Need for Speed (page 6)

Abracadabra (page 5)

Library Challenge (page 8)

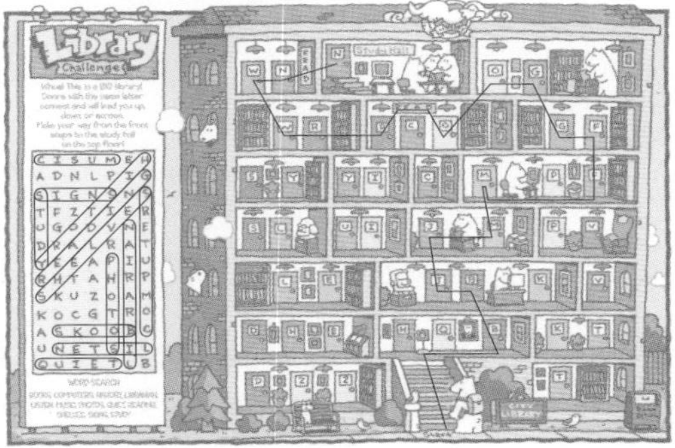

ANSWERS

Spaced Out (page 9)

SPACED OUT

A Day in the City (page 11)

LINK THE DOTS
ALL THE WAY UP IN THE SKY
Tallest
Shortest
BRIDGE MAZE
BRIDGE
CITY
FINISH
Where's the driver going, toward the city or the bridge? Have fun coloring him as you like!

Visitors from Outer Space (page 10)

VISITORS FROM
outer space
Connect the dots to draw the alien spaceship.
ALIENS
ARE OUT
OF THIS
WORLD
Use the code to solve this message.
What kind of pet would an alien get? Draw an alien pet below.

Tookie Bird Safari (page 12)

Tookie Bird Safari
START
Help the explorers find the sneaky Tookie Bird.
FINISH

ANSWERS

What's the Message? (page 14)

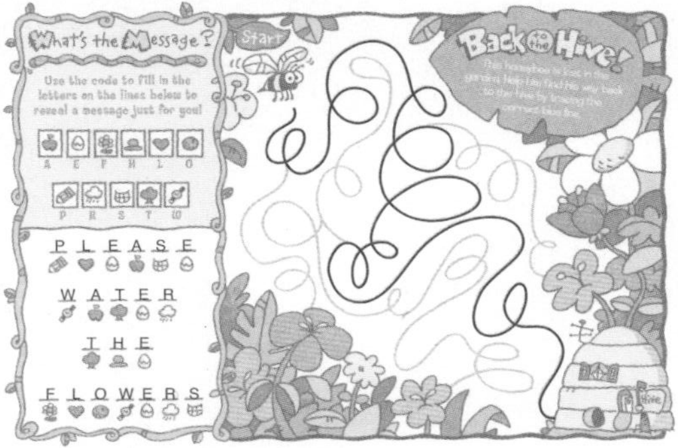
What's the Message?
Use the code to fill in the letters on the lines below to reveal a message just for you!
A E F H L O
P R S T W
PLEASE
WATER
THE
FLOWERS
Start
Back to the Hive!
Hive

The Wild West (page 16)

The Wild West
Which hat appears the most along this border?
Which of these two rootin'-tootin' cowpokes roped the moon? Who roped the sun?

Let's Make a Pizza! (page 15)

LET'S MAKE A PIZZA!

Go for the Goal! (page 18)

Go for the Goal!

ANSWERS

Oh Mummy! (page 19)

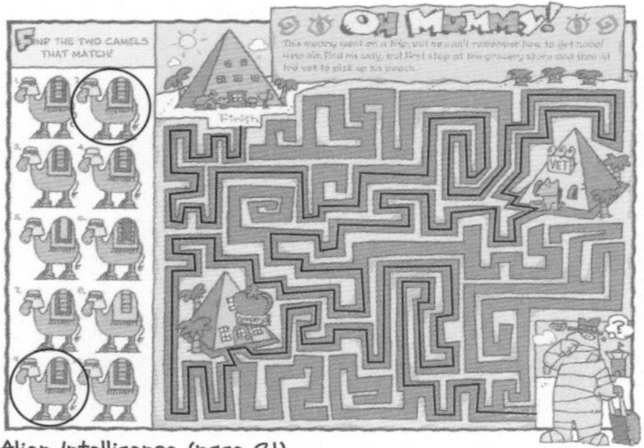
OH MUMMY!
FIND THE TWO CAMELS THAT MATCH!
Finish
VET

Big Top Challenge! (page 22)

BIG TOP
challenge!
THE FLYING BEARS ARE READY TO PERFORM, BUT ONE OF THEIR MEMBERS IS STILL ON THE GROUND! HELP THIS BEAR CHOOSE THE RIGHT ROPE FOR HIS CLIMB UP TOP!
NO WAY
Find

Alien Intelligence (page 21)

ALIEN INTELLIGENCE

In the Age of Dinosaurs (page 23)

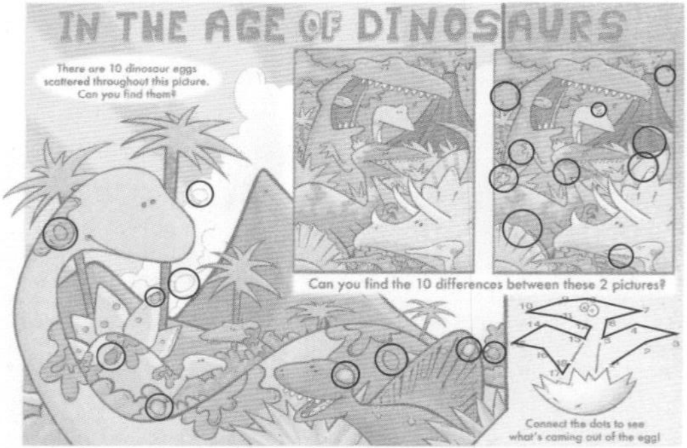
IN THE AGE OF DINOSAURS
There are 10 dinosaur eggs scattered throughout this picture. Can you find them?
Can you find the 10 differences between these 2 pictures?
Connect the dots to see what's coming out of the egg!

ANSWERS

Up in the Sky! (page 24)

Fe-Fi-Fo-Fum! (page 26)

Help this poor giant get his goose back from that **thievin' Jack!**

Unscramble these **Fairy-Tale Folks!**

AREDILNELC	Cinderella
EEN ACTTIH TRELEP TTLIG	The Three Little Pigs
LEPAGINES TYBEAU	Sleeping Beauty
TREEP NAP	Peter Pan
HOINCOCIP	Pinocchio
OWNSD TIHEW	Snow White
TEHMOR GEOSCE	Mother Goose
YTHALM PUDYMH	Humpty Dumpty
EHT BIG DAB OLWE	The Big Bad Wolf

Time to Dine! (page 25)

Creepy Crawlies (page 28)

ANSWERS

The Great Dino Cookie Chase (page 29)

The Great Dino COOKIE CHASE
Start
Finish

TreeHouse Maze-o-Rama (page 32)

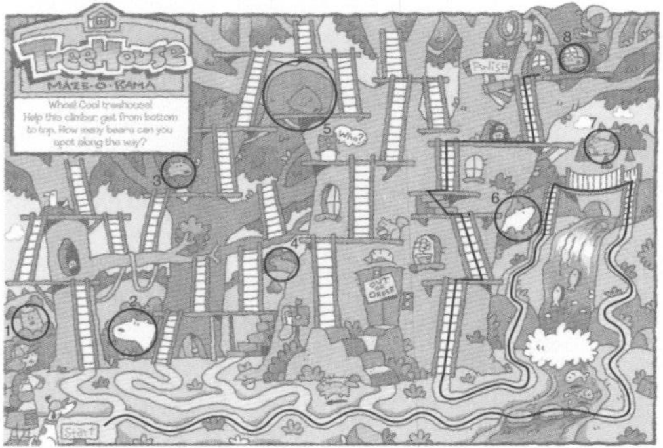
TreeHouse MAZE-O-RAMA
Whoa! Cool treehouse! Help this climber get from bottom to top. How many bears can you spot along the way?
FINISH
Who?
OUT OF ORDER
Start

Fun at the Beach (page 30)

Fun AT THE Beach

A Trip to the Zoo (page 33)

YIKES! THE ANIMALS HAVE TAKEN LETTERS FROM SIGNS AROUND THE ZOO! PLEASE MATCH THE LETTER TO EACH ANIMAL IN THE BLANKS TO ANSWER THIS QUESTION: WHAT DO DOLPHINS WEAR TO KEEP WARM?
A Trip to the Zoo
F L I P P E R S L I P P E R S
CAN YOU FIND THE ONE CAMEL THAT MATCHES THIS SHADOW EXACTLY?
CHANGE ONE LETTER PER WORD TO TRANSFORM THIS SWEET LITTLE DEER INTO A FEROCIOUS LION!!
DEER
DEAR TERM OF AFFECTION
LEAR SHAKESPEARE KING
LEAN TO REST ON
LOAN TO LEND MONEY
LOON LARGE WATERBIRD
LION

ANSWERS

A Day at the Museum (page 34)

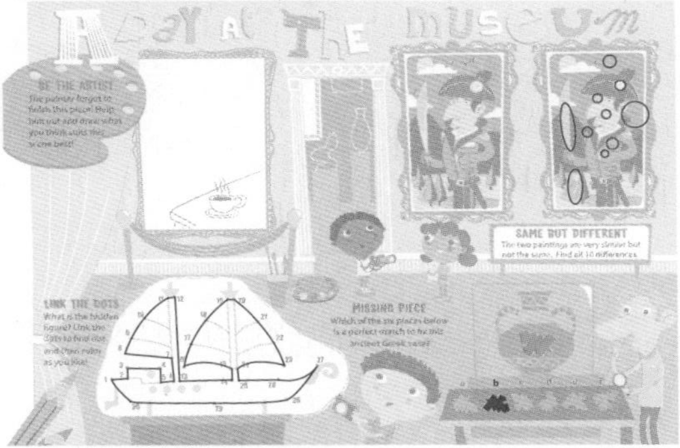

Road Trip Maze (page 36)

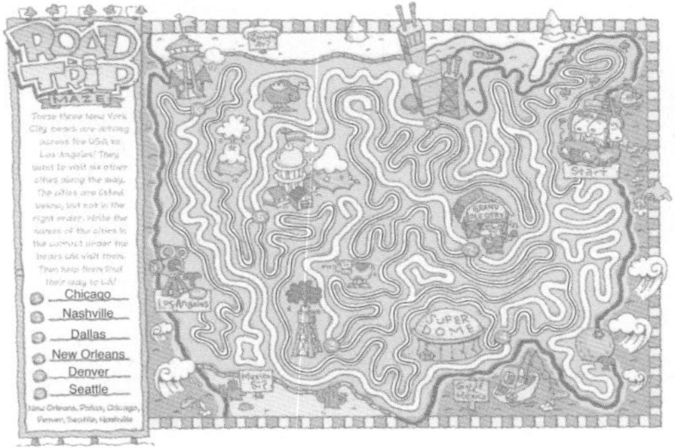

Monster Maker (page 35)

Snow Day! (page 37)

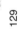

ANSWERS

At the Pet Shop (page 38)

Dino Dots (page 41)

A Day at the Zoo (page 40)

Polar Playtime (page 42)

ANSWERS

Pumpkin Patch Challenge (page 43)

Pumpkin Patch Challenge
We found our pumpkins! Now help us get through the patch and the corn maze to the EXIT!
START
CORN MAZE
Oops
EXIT

Sea Surprise (page 45)

SEA SURPRISE

Under the Sea (page 44)

Under the Sea
Find these objects in the crusty coral.
net
bubble
hook
worm
boot
There are five pairs of matching fish. Can you spot them?
Help Gil the Guppy get home to his wife, Gillian.
START
FINISH

On the Farm (page 47)

ON THE FARM
It's dinnertime! Help Bessie back to the barn.
START
FINISH

ANSWERS

Fun in the Park (page 48)

FUN IN THE
PARK

Pasta-Mania (page 50)

PASTA-MANIA
Mama Mia, that's a lot of spaghetti! Find your way from our hungry eater to the spicy meatball at the end!
YUM!
FINISH

Gym Class (page 49)

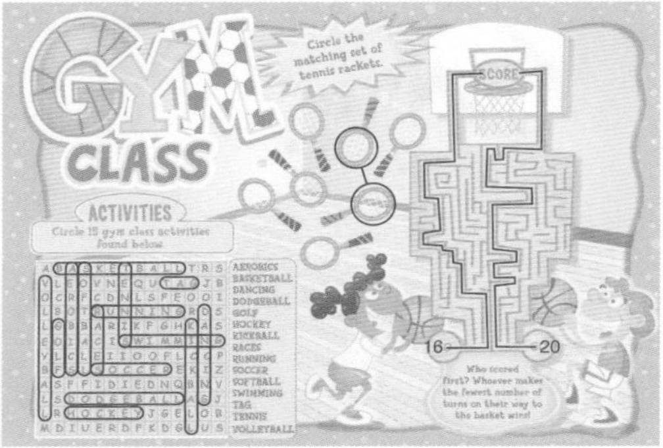
GYM CLASS
Circle the matching set of tennis rackets.
ACTIVITIES
Circle 15 gym class activities found below
AEROBICS
BASKETBALL
DANCING
DODGEBALL
GOLF
HOCKEY
KICKBALL
RACES
RUNNING
SOCCER
SOFTBALL
SWIMMING
TAG
TENNIS
VOLLEYBALL
SCORE
16
20
Who scored first? Whoever makes the fewest number of turns on their way to the basket wins!

Going Underground (page 52)

GOING UNDERGROUND

ANSWERS

Where's Charlie? (page 53)

The Water Park (page 55)

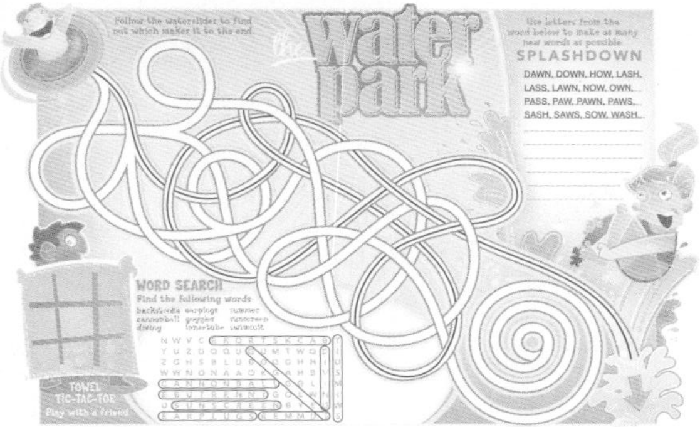

Treasure Hunt (page 54)

Mad for Mexico (page 56)

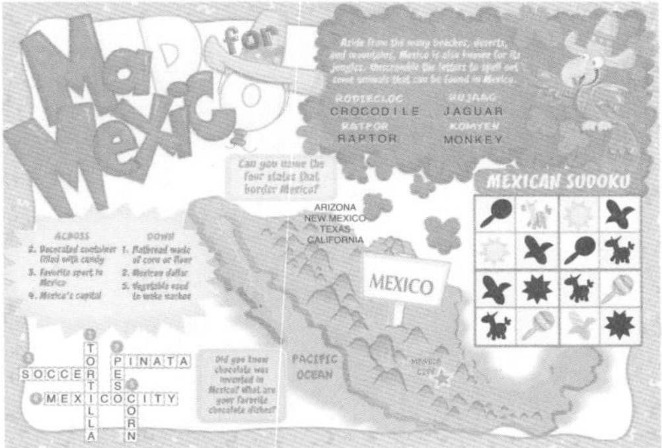

ANSWERS

Life on the Farm (page 57)

LIFE ON THE FARM

Museums Are Dino-Mite! (page 60)

MUSEUMS ARE DINO-MITE!

Castle Rescue (page 59)

Castle Rescue
The princess is trapped in the castle tower! Help the noble knight find his way to rescue her, and then unscramble these words:
DRAGON
CASTLE
PRINCESS
KNIGHT
KINGDOM
MOAT
SWORD

Jungle Exploration (page 61)

JUNGLE EXPLORATION
CAN YOU HELP THE MIGHTY JUNGLE MAN GET HOME SO HE CAN ENJOY A DELICIOUS BANANA SHAKE?!!
SNAKES!
PIRANHAS!
MMM - DELICIOUS BANANA SHAKE!

ANSWERS

Rover's Lost! (page 62)

Rover's Lost!
Oh, no! Rover has wandered off again, and he can't remember how to get back. Help him find his way home for dinner. Then solve these word puzzles.
birdhouse
eyeglasses
moonlight
dogcatcher
ROVER!

Pirates! (page 64)

Pirates!!
There are 14 bones hidden in the picture. Find them or walk the plank!
There are 20 things in this picture that start with a "p". Can you find them?

Mini Golf (page 63)

There's only one path that leads to the hole. Which one is it, 1, 2, or 3? Help the player find the right one!

Pirate Puzzle (page 66)

Pirate Puzzle

ANSWERS

Quest for Fuel (page 67)

QUEST for FUEL
START
FUEL
FINISH

Antarctica Adventure (page 69)

ANTARCTICA ADVENTURE
Help Ziggy cross the floating ice so he can get to his mom.
START
END
Unscramble the letters below to find out what it's like in Antarctica.
FEZINEGR DOLC
FREEZING COLD

Comic Book Heroes (page 68)

COMIC BOOK HEROES
Help this hero find his way through this maze to catch the bandit.
Unscramble the letters to discover what many comic book heroes have.
CESTER NITTYEDI
SECRET IDENTITY
Find the five hidden masks on this page.
START
Find the eight things a comic book hero might have.
ARCHENEMY
CAPE
COSTUME
GADGETS
LOGO
MASK
POWERS
TRAITS

Join ye Dots (page 70)

Join ye Dots

ANSWERS

School Map (page 72)

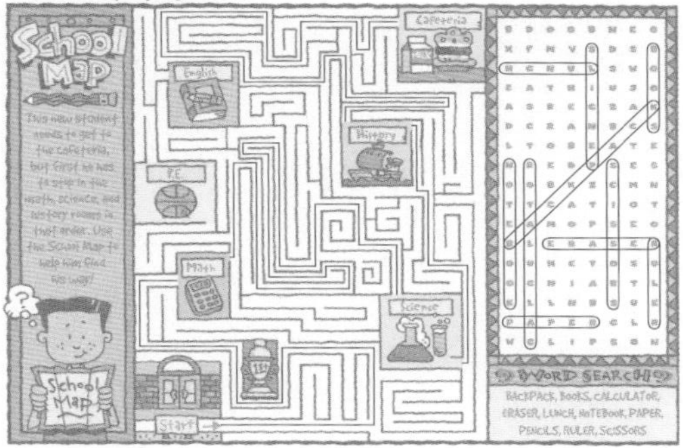

Monster Bash (page 73)

Mummy Mia! (page 74)

Gone Fishin' (page 75)

ANSWERS

Holiday Cruise (page 76)

Downhill Run (page 79)

Robots! (page 78)

Get to Gramma's House! (page 81)

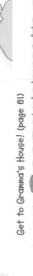

ANSWERS

Growing Green (page 83)

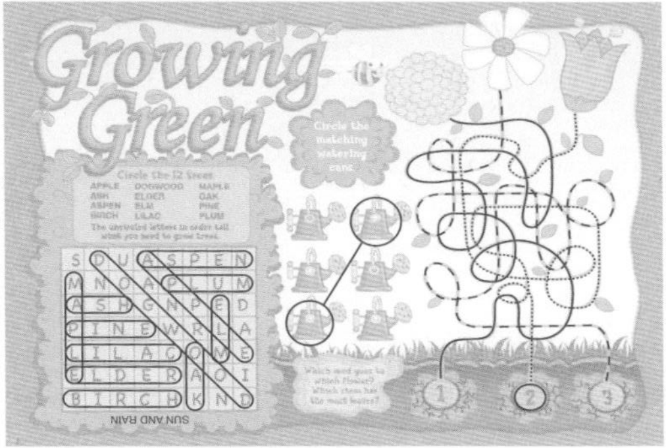

Fishy Friends (page 85)

Join the Dots (page 84)

Trip to Egypt (page 87)

ANSWERS

Sightseeing in Paris (page 88)

Sightseeing in Paris
METRO

Happy Landings! (page 92)

Happy Landings!

Everest Challenge (page 90)

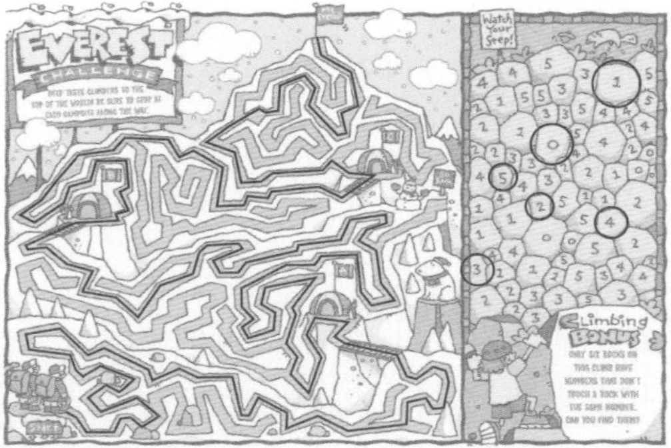

EVEREST
CHALLENGE
Watch Your Step!
Climbing Bonus

Across the USA (page 93)

Across the USA
Unscramble the letters below to spell out the names of seven states.
OLDACORO COLORADO
TUAH UTAH
ARILFOD FLORIDA
AGIMCHIN MICHIGAN
SATEX TEXAS
GERNOO OREGON
NORAZIA ARIZONA
Which two states do not touch any other states?
Alaska
Hawaii
Hint: Which city is called "The Windy City"?
Which state is the "Sunshine State"?
Florida
Which city is called "The Big Apple"?
New York City

ANSWERS

Ride 'em Cowboy! (page 96)

Ride 'em Cowboy!

Good Luck! (page 99)

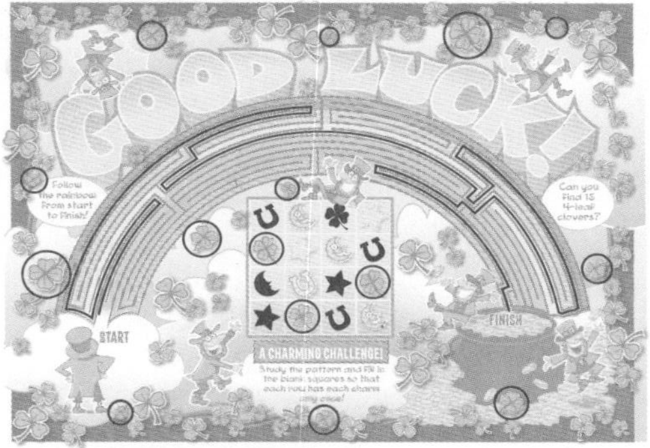
GOOD LUCK!
Follow the rainbow from start to finish!
Can you find 15 4-leaf clovers?
START
FINISH
A CHARMING CHALLENGE!
Study the pattern and fill in the blank squares so that each row has each charm only once!

Day at the Ballgame (page 98)

SCORE A SNACK!
CHIPS
HOTDOG
ICECREAM
FRIES
PRETZEL
PEANUTS
NACHOS
Fill in the spaces above with the names of the snacks below. Then read the secret phrase in the middle.
BALLGAME
Find 12 objects that don't belong on the ballfield.
Fill in the blanks to spell the names of baseball teams. Then unscramble the circled letters and fill in the umpire's phrase.
CARDINALS
MARLINS
PHILLIES
BRAVES
YANKEES
RANGERS
PLAY BALL

African Savanna (page 100)

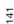

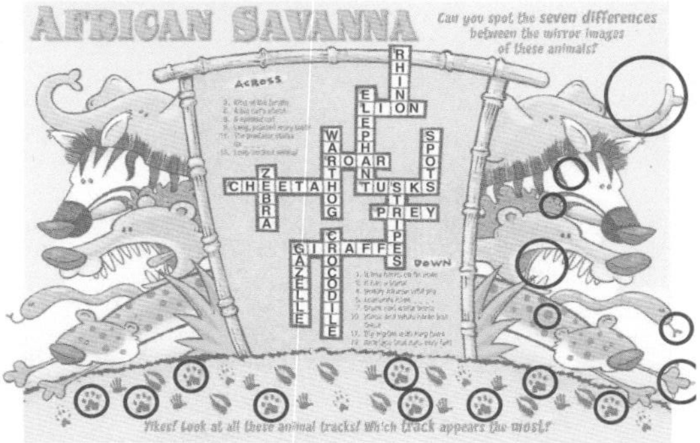
AFRICAN SAVANNA
Can you spot the seven differences between the mirror images of these animals?
Across
Down
RHINO
LION
ELEPHANT
WARTHOG
ROAR
SPOTS
CHEETAH
ZEBRA
TUSKS
STRIPES
PREY
GIRAFFE
GAZELLE
CROCODILE
Yikes! Look at all these animal tracks! Which track appears the most?

ANSWERS

On Safari (page 102)

Train Trip (page 105)

Going Buggy! (page 103)

Parade! (page 106)

ANSWERS

City Skyline (page 108)

CITY SKYLINE

Ridin' the Rails (page 114)

RIDIN' THE RAILS

Rodeo Fun (page 112)

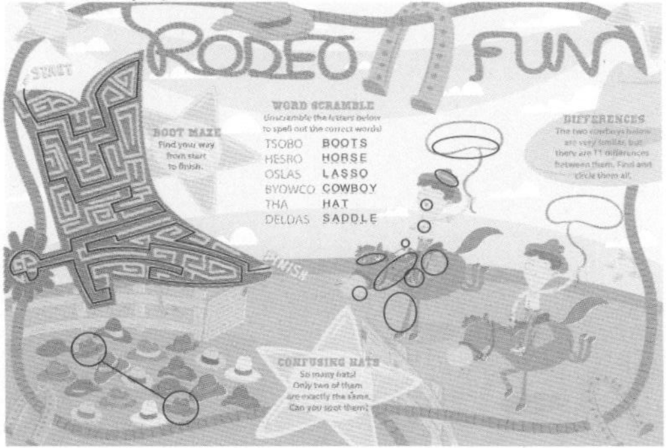
RODEO FUN
START
BOOT MAZE
Find your way from start to finish.
FINISH
WORD SCRAMBLE
Unscramble the letters below to spell out the correct words
TSOBO BOOTS
HESRO HORSE
OSLAS LASSO
BYOWCO COWBOY
THA HAT
DELDAS SADDLE
DIFFERENCES
The two cowboys below are very similar, but there are 11 differences between them. Find and circle them all.
CONFUSING HATS
So many hats! Only two of them are exactly the same. Can you spot them?

Haunted House (page 116)

HAUNTED HOUSE
JEEPERS CREEPERS! CAN YOU FIND THE EXACT MIRROR IMAGE OF THIS GHOST?!!
PLEASE FIND THESE SPOOKY WORDS IN THE WORD SEARCH ABOVE!
BOO CREAK CREEPY FANGS FRANKENSTEIN
GHOST GHOUL GOBLIN MONSTER MUMMY
SKELETON VAMPIRE WEREWOLF WITCH ZOMBIE
YIKES!! THERE ARE 20 SPIDERS LURKING ABOUT- CAN YOU FIND THEM ALL?!!

ANSWERS

Trip to New York (page 117)

Splish Splash (page 120)

Visit the Museum Maze (page 119)